WHEN YOU'RE SANE

(A Finn Wright FBI Suspense Thriller—Book Five)

BLAKE PIERCE

Blake Pierce

Blake Pierce is the USA Today bestselling author of the RILEY PAGE mystery series, which includes seventeen books. Blake Pierce is also the author of the MACKENZIE WHITE mystery series, comprising fourteen books; of the AVERY BLACK mystery series, comprising six books; of the KERI LOCKE mystery series, comprising five books; of the MAKING OF RILEY PAIGE mystery series, comprising six books; of the KATE WISE mystery series, comprising seven books; of the CHLOE FINE psychological suspense mystery, comprising six books; of the JESSIE HUNT psychological suspense thriller series, comprising thirty-five books (and counting); of the AU PAIR psychological suspense thriller series, comprising three books; of the ZOE PRIME mystery series, comprising six books; of the ADELE SHARP mystery series, comprising sixteen books, of the EUROPEAN VOYAGE cozy mystery series, comprising six books; of the LAURA FROST FBI suspense thriller, comprising eleven books; of the ELLA DARK FBI suspense thriller, comprising twenty-one books (and counting); of the A YEAR IN EUROPE cozy mystery series, comprising nine books, of the AVA GOLD mystery series, comprising six books; of the RACHEL GIFT mystery series, comprising thirteen books (and counting); of the VALERIE LAW mystery series, comprising nine books; of the PAIGE KING mystery series, comprising eight books; of the MAY MOORE mystery series, comprising eleven books; of the CORA SHIELDS mystery series, comprising eight books; of the NICKY LYONS mystery series, comprising eight books, of the CAMI LARK mystery series, comprising ten books; of the AMBER YOUNG mystery series, comprising seven books (and counting); of the DAISY FORTUNE mystery series, comprising five books; of the FIONA RED mystery series, comprising eleven books (and counting); of the FAITH BOLD mystery series, comprising eleven books (and counting); of the JULIETTE HART mystery series, comprising five books (and counting); of the MORGAN CROSS mystery series, comprising nine books (and counting); of the FINN WRIGHT mystery series, comprising five books (and counting); of the new SHEILA STONE suspense thriller series, comprising five books (and counting); and of the new RACHEL BLACKWOOD suspense thriller series, comprising five books (and counting).

An avid reader and lifelong fan of the mystery and thriller genres, Blake loves to hear from you, so please feel free to visit www.blakepierceauthor.com to learn more and stay in touch.

Copyright © 2024 by Blake Pierce. All rights reserved. Except as permitted under the U.S. Copyright Act of 1976, no part of this publication may be reproduced, distributed or transmitted in any form or by any means, or stored in a database or retrieval system, without the prior permission of the author. This ebook is licensed for your personal enjoyment only. This ebook may not be re-sold or given away to other people. If you would like to share this book with another person, please purchase an additional copy for each recipient. If you're reading this book and did not purchase it, or it was not purchased for your use only, then please return it and purchase your own copy. Thank you for respecting the hard work of this author. This is a work of fiction. Names, characters, businesses, organizations, places, events, and incidents either are the product of the author's imagination or are used fictionally. Any resemblance to actual persons, living or dead, is entirely coincidental. Jacket image Copyright ecrafts used under license from Shutterstock.com.
ISBN: 978-1-0943-8425-2

BOOKS BY BLAKE PIERCE

RACHEL BLACKWOOD SUSPENSE THRILLER
NOT THIS WAY (Book #1)
NOT THIS TIME (Book #2)
NOT THIS CLOSE (Book #3)
NOT THIS ROAD (Book #4)
NOT THIS LATE (Book #5)

SHEILA STONE SUSPENSE THRILLER
SILENT GIRL (Book #1)
SILENT TRAIL (Book #2)
SILENT NIGHT (Book #3)
SILENT HOUSE (Book #4)
SILENT SCREAM (Book #5)

FINN WRIGHT MYSTERY SERIES
WHEN YOU'RE MINE (Book #1)
WHEN YOU'RE SAFE (Book #2)
WHEN YOU'RE CLOSE (Book #3)
WHEN YOU'RE SLEEPING (Book #4)
WHEN YOU'RE SANE (Book #5)

MORGAN CROSS MYSTERY SERIES
FOR YOU (Book #1)
FOR RAGE (Book #2)
FOR LUST (Book #3)
FOR WRATH (Book #4)
FOREVER (Book #5)
FOR US (Book #6)
FOR NOW (Book #7)
FOR ONCE (Book #8)
FOR ETERNITY (Book #9)

JULIETTE HART MYSTERY SERIES
NOTHING TO FEAR (Book #1)
NOTHING THERE (Book #2)
NOTHING WATCHING (Book #3)

NOTHING HIDING (Book #4)
NOTHING LEFT (Book #5)

FAITH BOLD MYSTERY SERIES
SO LONG (Book #1)
SO COLD (Book #2)
SO SCARED (Book #3)
SO NORMAL (Book #4)
SO FAR GONE (Book #5)
SO LOST (Book #6)
SO ALONE (Book #7)
SO FORGOTTEN (Book #8)
SO INSANE (Book #9)
SO SMITTEN (Book #10)
SO SIMPLE (Book #11)

FIONA RED MYSTERY SERIES
LET HER GO (Book #1)
LET HER BE (Book #2)
LET HER HOPE (Book #3)
LET HER WISH (Book #4)
LET HER LIVE (Book #5)
LET HER RUN (Book #6)
LET HER HIDE (Book #7)
LET HER BELIEVE (Book #8)
LET HER FORGET (Book #9)
LET HER TRY (Book #10)
LET HER PLAY (Book #11)

DAISY FORTUNE MYSTERY SERIES
NEED YOU (Book #1)
CLAIM YOU (Book #2)
CRAVE YOU (Book #3)
CHOOSE YOU (Book #4)
CHASE YOU (Book #5)

AMBER YOUNG MYSTERY SERIES
ABSENT PITY (Book #1)
ABSENT REMORSE (Book #2)
ABSENT FEELING (Book #3)
ABSENT MERCY (Book #4)

ABSENT REASON (Book #5)
ABSENT SANITY (Book #6)
ABSENT LIFE (Book #7)

CAMI LARK MYSTERY SERIES
JUST ME (Book #1)
JUST OUTSIDE (Book #2)
JUST RIGHT (Book #3)
JUST FORGET (Book #4)
JUST ONCE (Book #5)
JUST HIDE (Book #6)
JUST NOW (Book #7)
JUST HOPE (Book #8)
JUST LEAVE (Book #9)
JUST TONIGHT (Book #10)

NICKY LYONS MYSTERY SERIES
ALL MINE (Book #1)
ALL HIS (Book #2)
ALL HE SEES (Book #3)
ALL ALONE (Book #4)
ALL FOR ONE (Book #5)
ALL HE TAKES (Book #6)
ALL FOR ME (Book #7)
ALL IN (Book #8)

CORA SHIELDS MYSTERY SERIES
UNDONE (Book #1)
UNWANTED (Book #2)
UNHINGED (Book #3)
UNSAID (Book #4)
UNGLUED (Book #5)
UNSTABLE (Book #6)
UNKNOWN (Book #7)
UNAWARE (Book #8)

MAY MOORE SUSPENSE THRILLER
NEVER RUN (Book #1)
NEVER TELL (Book #2)
NEVER LIVE (Book #3)
NEVER HIDE (Book #4)

NEVER FORGIVE (Book #5)
NEVER AGAIN (Book #6)
NEVER LOOK BACK (Book #7)
NEVER FORGET (Book #8)
NEVER LET GO (Book #9)
NEVER PRETEND (Book #10)
NEVER HESITATE (Book #11)

PAIGE KING MYSTERY SERIES
THE GIRL HE PINED (Book #1)
THE GIRL HE CHOSE (Book #2)
THE GIRL HE TOOK (Book #3)
THE GIRL HE WISHED (Book #4)
THE GIRL HE CROWNED (Book #5)
THE GIRL HE WATCHED (Book #6)
THE GIRL HE WANTED (Book #7)
THE GIRL HE CLAIMED (Book #8)

VALERIE LAW MYSTERY SERIES
NO MERCY (Book #1)
NO PITY (Book #2)
NO FEAR (Book #3)
NO SLEEP (Book #4)
NO QUARTER (Book #5)
NO CHANCE (Book #6)
NO REFUGE (Book #7)
NO GRACE (Book #8)
NO ESCAPE (Book #9)

RACHEL GIFT MYSTERY SERIES
HER LAST WISH (Book #1)
HER LAST CHANCE (Book #2)
HER LAST HOPE (Book #3)
HER LAST FEAR (Book #4)
HER LAST CHOICE (Book #5)
HER LAST BREATH (Book #6)
HER LAST MISTAKE (Book #7)
HER LAST DESIRE (Book #8)
HER LAST REGRET (Book #9)
HER LAST HOUR (Book #10)
HER LAST SHOT (Book #11)

HER LAST PRAYER (Book #12)
HER LAST LIE (Book #13)

AVA GOLD MYSTERY SERIES
CITY OF PREY (Book #1)
CITY OF FEAR (Book #2)
CITY OF BONES (Book #3)
CITY OF GHOSTS (Book #4)
CITY OF DEATH (Book #5)
CITY OF VICE (Book #6)

A YEAR IN EUROPE
A MURDER IN PARIS (Book #1)
DEATH IN FLORENCE (Book #2)
VENGEANCE IN VIENNA (Book #3)
A FATALITY IN SPAIN (Book #4)

ELLA DARK FBI SUSPENSE THRILLER
GIRL, ALONE (Book #1)
GIRL, TAKEN (Book #2)
GIRL, HUNTED (Book #3)
GIRL, SILENCED (Book #4)
GIRL, VANISHED (Book 5)
GIRL ERASED (Book #6)
GIRL, FORSAKEN (Book #7)
GIRL, TRAPPED (Book #8)
GIRL, EXPENDABLE (Book #9)
GIRL, ESCAPED (Book #10)
GIRL, HIS (Book #11)
GIRL, LURED (Book #12)
GIRL, MISSING (Book #13)
GIRL, UNKNOWN (Book #14)
GIRL, DECEIVED (Book #15)
GIRL, FORLORN (Book #16)
GIRL, REMADE (Book #17)
GIRL, BETRAYED (Book #18)
GIRL, BOUND (Book #19)
GIRL, REFORMED (Book #20)
GIRL, REBORN (Book #21)

LAURA FROST FBI SUSPENSE THRILLER

ALREADY GONE (Book #1)
ALREADY SEEN (Book #2)
ALREADY TRAPPED (Book #3)
ALREADY MISSING (Book #4)
ALREADY DEAD (Book #5)
ALREADY TAKEN (Book #6)
ALREADY CHOSEN (Book #7)
ALREADY LOST (Book #8)
ALREADY HIS (Book #9)
ALREADY LURED (Book #10)
ALREADY COLD (Book #11)

EUROPEAN VOYAGE COZY MYSTERY SERIES
MURDER (AND BAKLAVA) (Book #1)
DEATH (AND APPLE STRUDEL) (Book #2)
CRIME (AND LAGER) (Book #3)
MISFORTUNE (AND GOUDA) (Book #4)
CALAMITY (AND A DANISH) (Book #5)
MAYHEM (AND HERRING) (Book #6)

ADELE SHARP MYSTERY SERIES
LEFT TO DIE (Book #1)
LEFT TO RUN (Book #2)
LEFT TO HIDE (Book #3)
LEFT TO KILL (Book #4)
LEFT TO MURDER (Book #5)
LEFT TO ENVY (Book #6)
LEFT TO LAPSE (Book #7)
LEFT TO VANISH (Book #8)
LEFT TO HUNT (Book #9)
LEFT TO FEAR (Book #10)
LEFT TO PREY (Book #11)
LEFT TO LURE (Book #12)
LEFT TO CRAVE (Book #13)
LEFT TO LOATHE (Book #14)
LEFT TO HARM (Book #15)
LEFT TO RUIN (Book #16)

THE AU PAIR SERIES
ALMOST GONE (Book#1)
ALMOST LOST (Book #2)

ALMOST DEAD (Book #3)

ZOE PRIME MYSTERY SERIES
FACE OF DEATH (Book#1)
FACE OF MURDER (Book #2)
FACE OF FEAR (Book #3)
FACE OF MADNESS (Book #4)
FACE OF FURY (Book #5)
FACE OF DARKNESS (Book #6)

A JESSIE HUNT PSYCHOLOGICAL SUSPENSE SERIES
THE PERFECT WIFE (Book #1)
THE PERFECT BLOCK (Book #2)
THE PERFECT HOUSE (Book #3)
THE PERFECT SMILE (Book #4)
THE PERFECT LIE (Book #5)
THE PERFECT LOOK (Book #6)
THE PERFECT AFFAIR (Book #7)
THE PERFECT ALIBI (Book #8)
THE PERFECT NEIGHBOR (Book #9)
THE PERFECT DISGUISE (Book #10)
THE PERFECT SECRET (Book #11)
THE PERFECT FAÇADE (Book #12)
THE PERFECT IMPRESSION (Book #13)
THE PERFECT DECEIT (Book #14)
THE PERFECT MISTRESS (Book #15)
THE PERFECT IMAGE (Book #16)
THE PERFECT VEIL (Book #17)
THE PERFECT INDISCRETION (Book #18)
THE PERFECT RUMOR (Book #19)
THE PERFECT COUPLE (Book #20)
THE PERFECT MURDER (Book #21)
THE PERFECT HUSBAND (Book #22)
THE PERFECT SCANDAL (Book #23)
THE PERFECT MASK (Book #24)
THE PERFECT RUSE (Book #25)
THE PERFECT VENEER (Book #26)
THE PERFECT PEOPLE (Book #27)
THE PERFECT WITNESS (Book #28)
THE PERFECT APPEARANCE (Book #29)
THE PERFECT TRAP (Book #30)

THE PERFECT EXPRESSION (Book #31)
THE PERFECT ACCOMPLICE (Book #32)
THE PERFECT SHOW (Book #33)
THE PERFECT POISE (Book #34)
THE PERFECT CROWD (Book #35)

CHLOE FINE PSYCHOLOGICAL SUSPENSE SERIES
NEXT DOOR (Book #1)
A NEIGHBOR'S LIE (Book #2)
CUL DE SAC (Book #3)
SILENT NEIGHBOR (Book #4)
HOMECOMING (Book #5)
TINTED WINDOWS (Book #6)

KATE WISE MYSTERY SERIES
IF SHE KNEW (Book #1)
IF SHE SAW (Book #2)
IF SHE RAN (Book #3)
IF SHE HID (Book #4)
IF SHE FLED (Book #5)
IF SHE FEARED (Book #6)
IF SHE HEARD (Book #7)

THE MAKING OF RILEY PAIGE SERIES
WATCHING (Book #1)
WAITING (Book #2)
LURING (Book #3)
TAKING (Book #4)
STALKING (Book #5)
KILLING (Book #6)

RILEY PAIGE MYSTERY SERIES
ONCE GONE (Book #1)
ONCE TAKEN (Book #2)
ONCE CRAVED (Book #3)
ONCE LURED (Book #4)
ONCE HUNTED (Book #5)
ONCE PINED (Book #6)
ONCE FORSAKEN (Book #7)
ONCE COLD (Book #8)
ONCE STALKED (Book #9)

ONCE LOST (Book #10)
ONCE BURIED (Book #11)
ONCE BOUND (Book #12)
ONCE TRAPPED (Book #13)
ONCE DORMANT (Book #14)
ONCE SHUNNED (Book #15)
ONCE MISSED (Book #16)
ONCE CHOSEN (Book #17)

MACKENZIE WHITE MYSTERY SERIES
BEFORE HE KILLS (Book #1)
BEFORE HE SEES (Book #2)
BEFORE HE COVETS (Book #3)
BEFORE HE TAKES (Book #4)
BEFORE HE NEEDS (Book #5)
BEFORE HE FEELS (Book #6)
BEFORE HE SINS (Book #7)
BEFORE HE HUNTS (Book #8)
BEFORE HE PREYS (Book #9)
BEFORE HE LONGS (Book #10)
BEFORE HE LAPSES (Book #11)
BEFORE HE ENVIES (Book #12)
BEFORE HE STALKS (Book #13)
BEFORE HE HARMS (Book #14)

AVERY BLACK MYSTERY SERIES
CAUSE TO KILL (Book #1)
CAUSE TO RUN (Book #2)
CAUSE TO HIDE (Book #3)
CAUSE TO FEAR (Book #4)
CAUSE TO SAVE (Book #5)
CAUSE TO DREAD (Book #6)

KERI LOCKE MYSTERY SERIES
A TRACE OF DEATH (Book #1)
A TRACE OF MURDER (Book #2)
A TRACE OF VICE (Book #3)
A TRACE OF CRIME (Book #4)
A TRACE OF HOPE (Book #5)

PROLOGUE

Lily's footsteps echoed in the vast entryway of the castle, the once grandiose space now a chaotic mix of vibrant and clashing colors. The ancient tapestries that once adorned the walls had in recent times been replaced with modern art pieces, the sharp angles and vivid hues making Lily uncomfortable. Since she had moved there, the history of the place was in the process of renovation, of being wiped from existence and replaced with eccentric designs her husband loved.

As she walked on the stone and marble floors, Lily could see fragments of the moonlight from the night sky catching the scaffolding, a monstrosity of its own, which climbed up the walls outside, casting long black shadows like fingers on the floor of the quiet castle.

As she wandered deeper into the castle's labyrinth of halls, rooms, and corridors, an eerie humming sound caught her attention. It seemed to come from nowhere and everywhere at once, sending a shiver down her spine. It was a noise she was not used to, certainly not at that time of night. She strained her ears, trying to pinpoint its origin. Was it the wind creeping through an open space due to all of the renovations? Machinery left on by accident by the workers, long since gone home for the night? It crossed Lily's mind that it seemed more malevolent than that.

"Thomas?" she called out, hoping her husband might be nearby. But her voice only echoed back at her, lost in the maze of rooms and hallways. A home she barely knew since their move from America, but one she felt did not appreciate her presence.

The strange noise continued to draw her in as she meandered through the castle. In one room, she caught glimpses of recent changes the decorators had carried out at her husband's behest. Some of the original stonework had been painted over with modern shapes and patterns like spirals, an odd addition which seemed almost sacrilegious. Lily wished they could just have enjoyed the castle for what it was, but her husband always believed that he had to leave a mark on a place.

The shadows around Lily seemed to grow with menace as she walked, and it felt as if the stones of the castle themselves were protesting, resisting the changes forced upon it.

She wondered if places had memories, or worse, intentions. And if the place had intentions, Lily, knowing quite well that was guilty of superstitious flights of fancy at the best of times, still worried that somehow the history of the castle itself might strike back at her and her husband for what they had done.

"Thomas? Darling?" she asked the night again, her voice wavering with unease as she continued through the castle.

She couldn't shake the feeling that something was off, that the humming sound was more than just an innocuous sound from a refrigerator unit or a generator left on by the workmen during the day. She tried to push her fears aside, telling herself it was simply an old pipe groaning within the aged walls.

"Where are you?" she whispered, her fingers brushing against the cool stone as she continued her search. The lack of response fueled a burning fear within, a growing sense of dread gnawing at her chest.

"Stop playing games, Thomas," she pleaded, knowing her husband's sometimes wicked sense of humor. "Answer me."

But almost-silence was all that greeted her, the insistent hum her only companion in the unsettling stillness. And though she didn't know what awaited her around each corner, she pressed on, a grim fear building inside of her with each step. Lily had hated being alone since she was a child. She had to find her husband in the darkness of the night, she refused to be alone with it.

Lily hesitated at the entrance to what should have been an old Victorian drawing room. The original wooden paneling lay in disarray, tossed aside haphazardly by the renovators before they'd left for the weekend. She sighed, regretting her decision not to retain any servants during the restoration process. At least that would have been company. The caretaker did live by in the nearest village, but he wasn't due to come around until the morning.

"Would've been nice to have a bit of company," she murmured, her voice barely audible above the persistent humming, which in places had become almost a howl.

Speaking to herself helped build the illusion that she had company, but a more dangerous type of company was what she feared most.

The sound seemed to be growing louder, beckoning her further into the castle.

As she stepped cautiously over the scattered debris, Lily found herself wishing they had stayed back in the US. Sure, it was her husband's dream to own an authentic English castle, but the isolation was beginning to take its toll on her nerves. How she missed her home where everything had made more sense to her.

Even if I were a ghost, I wouldn't want to stay here, she thought to herself with a shiver. For a moment, she wondered if the old stories about the castle being haunted were true.

She shook her head, trying to dispel the uneasy thoughts. It wasn't like her to get so easily spooked, but the eerie atmosphere and the unrelenting hum were getting under her skin.

"Get a grip, Lily," she whispered fiercely, clutching her arms for comfort. "It's just an old building, that's all."

But as she continued through the dimly lit corridors, her unease would not relent. A sense of being watched was beginning to cloud her mind, as though the darkness itself had eyes. And then, she stumbled upon something that made her blood run cold.

"Damn it!" she gasped, finding a window smashed, shards of glass littering the floor.

The broken window only fueled her fears – someone could have broken in. And with no one in the castle besides herself and her husband, the danger felt all too real. Lily began to fear that something had happened to Thomas.

She peered through the broken glass and saw that a piece of railing attached to the scaffolding had come loose, still hanging on by a worn piece of rope. It looked as though it had smashed the window, but Lily couldn't quite abandon the thought that human intervention was involved. That someone else was in the castle.

"Alright, think, Lily. What do you do now?" Her mind raced, considering her options.

Should she search for her husband, or go and phone the police? Her heart pounded in her chest as she weighed her choices. Then she imagined the police turning up in the middle of the night, looking at the scaffolding and chastising her for wasting police time. It would be embarrassing, and embarrassment was something Lily avoided like the plague. She had done this ever since she had been picked on at school as a young girl.

"This is silly," she decided, her voice wavering with determination. "There's no one else here but us."

Listening for a moment, Lily then followed the haunting howl, each step bringing her closer to whatever was making the noise.

An abrupt shift in the howl's pitch felt like a further warning. Just as she was about to dismiss it, her ears caught something worse – a scream. It pierced through the air like a siren, shrill and desperate. She froze, her breath hitching.

"Lily!" The cry echoed, making her heart clench with fear. It sounded like Thomas was indeed hurt.

"Coming!" Lily called out, adrenaline spiking as she bolted towards the stairs. Her mind rushed with the possibility that her husband had been drinking again. It had had happened once before, and she was now worried that he had banged his head or broken a leg.

Each step creaked beneath her feet, and each noise was an unwelcome companion. Her hands trembled as she gripped the banister at the bottom of another flight of stairs, forcing herself to climb despite every instinct screaming at her to flee.

"Thomas, where are you!?" She yelled, her voice cracking with panic. There was no response, only the sinister hum that seemed to mock her terror.

Lily hesitated outside an unassuming wooden door, feeling a sense of foreboding that chilled her to the bone. It was the library where Thomas had been spending an increasing amount of time. From behind it, the howl was at its most ferocious. Swallowing hard, she mustered up the courage to push it open. Immediately, she felt the icy coldness of the winter in that room, and she finally saw that another window was open, and the wind howled and pushed through it like a hungry predator.

But the howl was the least of her concerns.

Lily's eyes widened as they fell upon a horrifying sight – a dead man sprawled on the floor in a pool of crimson.

"Dear God, no!" she whimpered, her legs nearly buckling under the weight of her despair. With trembling hands, she reached out and touched the lifeless face. The cold, clammy skin confirmed her worst nightmare – it was her husband. It was her dear Thomas.

"T... Thomas!" she stammered, tears streaming down her cheeks as she choked out a scream of agony. Her vision blurred, but not enough to miss the shadow that suddenly burst from the corner of the room.

"Who's there?" she demanded, her voice wavering with fear. She squinted, trying to make out the figure holding something heavy, but the darkness obscured any identifying features.

"Help!" she shouted, raising her hands to defend herself. She turned towards the door. But it was in vain – the attacker lunged forward, bringing the object crashing down onto her head with an unnerving crunch.

Is this it? Lily's thoughts raced as she felt her skull crack under the assault. The pain was excruciating, yet all she could think about was who would save Thomas if he was still alive. And then, darkness swallowed her whole, and she slumped lifelessly to the ground.

The castle fell still once more, but for the strange howl, which continued to push through the open window in mocking laughter.

CHAPTER ONE

Finn Wright studied the hotel register in the dimly lit lobby with disquiet. He was not his usual jovial self. The stakes were too high for that.

The lobby was adorned with muted colors, tasteful furniture, and soft lighting that cast long shadows across the polished marble floors. The faint, what should have been soothing, sounds of a violin concerto played in the background.

Despite it being very early morning, the winter outside remained gloomy and only threatening daylight. His eyes traced over the cursive letters in the register, forming a name he knew all too well.

"Is everything alright, sir?" asked the receptionist, her voice crisp but tinged with concern.

"Uh, yes, thank you," Finn replied, forcing a smile. But as his gaze remained fixated on the signature, he knew things were far from okay.

It had been weeks since he had begun tracking Max Vilne, an escaped serial killer from the US who had somehow managed to elude him until now. Finn had put Vilne away once before. Going against orders, Finn had gone into a hotel alone to rescue one of Vilne's hostages. This confrontation nearly took the hotel with it, and although Finn rescued the hostage in the end and arrested Vilne, the hotel suffered millions of dollars worth of damage. This combined with his defying of orders, resulted in Finn's suspension from the FBI. Those events had brought Finn's professional life crumbling down, and if it weren't for a stroke of luck during a struggle, he knew that he wouldn't have made it out of there alive.

Vilne was a genius serial killer whom Finn hoped he'd never encounter again.

But somehow he had escaped and come to the UK, most likely for revenge. How he had made it that far across the Atlantic was still a mystery and a deep concern for the British Home Office, which Finn now worked with as a consultant detective.

Finn had studied Max's handwriting so thoroughly that he would never forget it. But the worry was that Vilne should have known that. Finn feared that Vilne had refused any attempt to cover up his handwriting, and that could only mean more danger than ever.

He stepped away from the reception desk, discreetly snapping a photo of the register page with his cell phone. He withdrew to a quiet corner near a potted fern and dialed Rob, his friend and Chief Inspector with the Hertfordshire Constabulary.

"Rob, it's Finn," he said, his voice low and urgent. "I've found Max Vilne. I'm sure of it."

"Where are you?" Rob asked, his tone instantly serious.

"Staying at a hotel in Croftwake. He signed the register not two hours ago."

"Finn, please," Rob said with concern. "That's not that far from the Constabulary building. Wait for Amelia and backup. Don't do anything rash. It's too dangerous."

"Can't afford to wait, Rob," Finn replied, his jaw set in determination. "If he gets away because I didn't do anything, then the next death is on me."

As much as he respected Rob and appreciated the camaraderie they shared, he couldn't let this opportunity slip through his fingers. The thought of Max causing more pain and suffering fueled his resolve. "I have to end this now."

"Listen to me, Finn—" Rob started, but Finn hung up before he could finish, the silence of the terminated call echoing in his ears. He knew Rob meant well, but this was something he had to do.

Finn pocketed his cell phone and took a deep breath, mentally preparing himself for what lay ahead. He caught his reflection in a large ornate mirror in the lobby. He realized he wasn't as well kept as he once was. His blond beard hadn't been trimmed in a while, and the dark patches under his eyes spoke of countless nights looking for a trail of breadcrumbs. The weight of his past, his suspension from the agency, the civil court case – all of it paled in comparison to the task at hand. This was his chance to make things right, and he wouldn't let anything stand in his way.

As he strode towards the elevator, he felt an odd mix of fear and finality. But he knew that Max Vilne would not simply surrender without a fight. And Finn would be ready for him, no matter the cost.

Finn's footsteps deadened on the plush carpet as he made his way to the elevator, his instincts sharpening with every step. The hotel was a tasteful blend of modern and traditional design, its high ceilings and expansive windows allowing for an abundance of natural light. Yet, despite the inviting atmosphere, Finn couldn't shake off the icy grip of trepidation.

The elevator doors slid shut, and as the metal box ascended, Finn steeled himself, his mind racing through potential scenarios and contingencies. The last time he had faced Vilne back in the US, he had come close to meeting his maker. Finn knew that he had been very lucky. But luck, like life, could run out at any moment.

"Room 405," he whispered under his breath, the numbers feeling like a countdown to an inevitable confrontation.

Upon reaching the fourth floor, Finn cautiously approached room 405, his senses heightened. He hesitated only for a moment before knocking firmly on the door. He used the fake name Vilne had given on the register: "Mr Carlton, sorry to bother you," Finn said, trying his best to mimic a generic English accent. "But we've had a leak coming through on the third floor, and we're having to check each room. I just need to look at the bathroom and make sure there are no leaking pipes in your room."

"Come in," Max Vilne's voice called out from behind the door, eerily calm and composed. Finn's blood almost froze at the sound of it.

"Keep it together, Finn," he muttered to himself as he opened the door and stepped inside.

The room was dimly lit, curtains drawn to obscure him from any prying eyes. Max stood near the window, his dim shape only accentuating the darkness in his eyes. He turned to face Finn, a cold smile playing on his lips.

To Finn, it was the face of Evil incarnate.

"Ah, Finn Wright. I've been enjoying my stay in your lovely adopted country," Max said casually, folding his arms across his chest. "I must say, your British friends do know how to make a serial killer feel welcome."

"Vilne!" Finn snapped, fists clenched at his sides. How he wished he was allowed to carry a firearm in the United Kingdom. He didn't have that safety net. But still, he had to go through with the confrontation. "You're under arrest."

"Am I?" Max replied, raising an eyebrow. "Now that's interesting. I think you'll find that it is you who are trapped."

Before Finn could react, Max flicked his wrist, throwing a handful of powder into Finn's face. The air around him became a suffocating cloud, burning his nostrils and throat. He choked and sputtered, desperately trying to draw in a breath. His vision blurred, and the room spun out of focus.

"Vilne..." Finn gasped, his knees buckling as he collapsed onto the floor.

"Sorry, old friend," Max taunted, standing over Finn's prone form. "You'll have to do better than this. You got me once through sheer luck, but now you must see how truly *weak* you are in comparison to me."

As the world faded away, Finn clung to the single thought that fueled his determination: He would not let Max Vilne win – no matter what it took.

With Max's sinister grin hovering above him, Finn could feel the weight of his own helplessness. The room continued to spin as dizziness clouded his senses. He tried to throw an upward punch, but his limbs were too heavy to lift.

"Quite a nifty little concoction I made at the chemists, don't you think?" Max gloated. "It'll wear off soon enough, but by then, I'll be long gone. The question is, will I have finished you off before leaving?" He let out a snide laugh.

Finn struggled to regain control of his body, his fingers digging into the carpet, but the powder's effects held him in its grasp.

"Death is too good for you. Your time will come, but not yet. Your life will become a living hell, Finn," Max whispered, leaning down close enough for Finn to feel his breath on his face. "You should have left well enough alone back home. But now, I want everyone to know how pathetic and useless you are. You can't even protect your loved ones."

The sound of rushing footsteps echoed through the hallway beyond the door, and Finn's heart clenched with both hope and dread. Max's smile widened, a gleam of malevolence in his eyes.

"Ah, sounds like a woman's gait. Could it be that the fiery redhead you've been keeping company with has come to rescue you? Inspector Winters, isn't it?" Max mused, watching Finn's reaction closely.

Finn knew that if it was Amelia, there was nothing he could do to protect her while drugged.

"I can see she matters to you," Max Vilne continued. "That's good of you to let me know. I'll add her to my list."

"Leave her out of this," Finn growled through gritted teeth, frustration boiling inside him.

"Can't make any promises, old friend," Max chuckled before swiftly moving towards the window. "I really just wanted you to know what you were in for, but I wonder if I should focus on this Winters woman rather than your ex-fiance Demi? See you soon." He threw the window open and slipped outside, disappearing from sight just as the door burst open.

The footsteps Finn had heard, did indeed belong to Amelia and two uniformed officers, who stood ready for a fight. They scanned the room, their eyes landing on Finn's prone form.

"Damn it, Finn," Amelia muttered, kneeling beside him and helping him sit up. She sounded angry, but but beneath it was simmering concern and affection. "We told you to wait for backup... Are you okay? What happened?"

"He drugged me... Max Vilne...he's gone," Finn managed to say, the room still spinning around him.

"I'll get an ambulance," Amelia said, her expression filled with care.

"I... I'm okay... I think it's temporary, just enough for him to toy with me. He made escaped through the window."

"Check the roof!" Amelia ordered the officers, who immediately rushed back out.

Finn fought off the dizziness, forcing himself to stand as the drug began to lose its grip on him.

"Amelia, it's no use," he insisted, his unsteady hand gripping her arm. "He's gone. He knew I was coming. He would have planned a meticulous escape."

Her eyes, filled with concern and frustration, met his for a moment before she nodded tersely. "We might get lucky. Even Vilne is capable of a mistake."

But soon the officers returned, shaking their heads at the lack of any sign of the killer. Finn's attention was drawn to an envelope on the table nearby as he now stood tall once more. His name stared back at him, written in Max's unmistakable scrawl. Finn didn't want to open it, but he had to.

With reluctance, he opened it, his mind racing with possible implications.

"You took what was mine, now I will take what is yours."

The words seemed to leap off the page, searing themselves into Finn's brain. Vilne talked about people like they were belongings, things to trifle with. Finn could only assume that Vilne was referring to Nancy Miller, the woman he saved from Vilne's clutches back in the US. Finn had stopped him from killing that time, and it had seemingly consumed Vilne ever since.

Now, he was going to take it out on Finn's loved ones.

Finn crumpled the paper in his fist, fury and fear intertwining within him. Max had made this personal, and Finn would not let him succeed. He would protect those he cared about, no matter the cost.

"Is everything alright?" Amelia asked, her voice laced with worry as she eyed the balled-up letter.

"Max left us a message," Finn replied, anger simmering beneath his words. "He's targeting the people I care about."

"Then let's make sure he doesn't get the chance," Amelia said firmly, her resolve shining through. "We'll put constables on high alert and have them protect anyone you need."

Finn nodded, his thoughts consumed by the chilling words of Max's taunt. The game had changed, and the stakes were higher than ever, but there was no end in sight, and Vilne seemed to be playing from a marked deck.

Amelia's phone shattered the tense silence, its shrill ring echoing off the walls of the hotel room. She glanced at Finn before pulling the device from her pocket and answering the call.

"Inspector Winters," she said, her tone crisp and professional as she listened to the voice on the other end. Finn watched her expression shift from concern to surprise, her eyebrows knitting together.

"Chief?" she said, holding up a hand as if to physically halt the barrage of information coming through the line. "Are you saying there's been another..." Her eyes widened, and she cast a sidelong glance at Finn. "Yes, alright. We'll be there as soon as we can."

"Was that Rob?" Finn asked, his stomach clenching with a sense of foreboding as he registered Amelia's reaction to the call.

"Home office wants us on a murder case," she said. "And they think it might be connected to Max Vilne. If we can't find Vilne here and track him down..."

"Then we follow the breadcrumbs wherever they lead," Finn said.

CHAPTER TWO

Finn still felt his breathing wasn't quite right as he and Amelia stepped into the spacious office of Chief Constable Rob Collins, sunlight streaming through the large windows overlooking the Hertfordshire Constabulary HQ. The warm glow illuminated the room, casting shadows on the shelves filled with case files and awards.

Finn was determined to hide how ill he was feeling after being drugged. He knew Rob would force him to step down, otherwise.

"Rob," Finn said, offering a weak smile to his old friend. Amelia nodded her head, addressing him as "Chief" in her usual respectful tone.

Rob was an old college friend, the very reason Finn had come to the UK in the first place on vacation. Now, he'd been there in the UK for nearly a whole year, living in Rob's aunt's vacant cottage, and making a name for himself in the press as a detective of peerless excellence.

But Finn wondered whether Rob truly knew how much jeopardy he was now in by being part of Finn's closest circle.

"Have a seat," Rob gestured to the chairs in front of his desk. As they settled into the worn leather seats, Rob scrutinized Finn, concern etched on his face. "You look like hell, mate. Have you slept at all?"

"Sleep? I hear it's lovely," Finn's voice trailed off, his gaze lost in the depths of his coffee cup. "I'm fine. I just need to catch Max Vilne."

"Any sightings since this morning?" Amelia asked, the urgency in her voice unmistakable.

"None," Rob replied, shuffling through a stack of papers on his desk. "Max Vilne hasn't been seen since he escaped the hotel room. It appears he had tied a rope to the next building's roof in anticipation of a quick escape. Then, he cut the rope so our constables couldn't follow. By the time we had constables combing the area, he was long gone. Not even a sighting on CCTV, which makes me think he had scouted them out in advance. He's quite the slippery fellow... It's likely he's gone dark again."

Finn rubbed his temples, trying to suppress the headache that had been lurking at the edges of his consciousness. He could feel the weight of the past pressing down on him, the memories of his suspension and the end of his relationship with Demi threatening to consume him.

"Rob," Finn's voice cracked, betraying his exhaustion. "I'm worried about Demi. And Amelia and your safety, too. Max has a terrible grudge against me because I put him away."

"Trust me, Finn, we're taking every precaution," Rob assured him, his voice calm and steady. "But you know as well as I do that Max Vilne is a master at evading capture. We won't let our guard down, I can assure you."

Finn's eyes darted around the room, seeking reassurance in the familiar surroundings. It was never easy for him to ask for help, but he knew that Amelia and Rob were the only people he could trust.

"Rob, what can we do?" Finn asked, desperation tingeing his question. "We have to find him before he gets to Demi, or... Anyone else." Finn didn't want to say that he had Amelia on his mind most of all. They all meant the world to him, but Amelia was... He didn't quite know what, but he knew this much – his feelings for her were growing by the day.

"Demi is safe and under our protection, so don't worry," Rob said, leaning forward in his chair, determination lighting up his eyes. "We need to follow the trail of this new case. It might be our best chance to catch Max Vilne."

"Let's hope so," Finn muttered, standing up from his chair. "Because if we don't, there's no telling what kind of devastation he'll cause."

The oppressive atmosphere of Rob's office seemed to close in on Finn, making it harder for him to breathe. He caught Amelia watching him for a moment with her deep green eyes.

"Look, Finn," Amelia said, her voice firm but gentle. "You can't keep working yourself like this. I'd like to suggest that I do this case on my own... Just the initial evaluation so you can get some rest, and..."

"No," Finn said, firmly.

"Amelia's right," Rob added, nodding in agreement. "You need some rest. I understand why you feel the need to catch Vilne. It might be our only lead, but..."

"Exactly," Finn replied, clenching his fists. "I'm not going anywhere until this is done. So what's the story?"

"Finn, please," Amelia said, softly.

Rob leaned back in his chair and sighed. "I know when not to argue with Finn Wright, Amelia. Okay, Finn. It's your dance. A wealthy American named Thomas Richmond was found murdered in a castle he recently purchased here in Hertfordshire, alongside the body of his wife, Lily Richmond. The Home Office believes there may be a connection to Max Vilne due to the proximity to his last known location and the fact that the victim is an American citizen."

Finn narrowed his eyes as he processed the information.

"I don't know, Chief. The connection to Max Vilne seems tenuous at best," Amelia answered. "I'm worried we might be putting our energy into a case that has nothing to do with him.

"True," Rob admitted, leaning back in his chair and steepling his fingers. "But there is another theory that I've thought of. We're not certain how Vilne managed to get to the UK after escaping prison in America. How did he do it without getting caught? It seems an awful gamble to have used a plane. But consider this: Thomas Richmond, our victim, owned a company that transports goods between the US and the UK. It's plausible that Vilne could've used Richmond's services to make his way here."

Finn nodded in agreement. "You think Richmond smuggled Vilne into the country, and then Vilne killed him to cover his tracks?"

"Nothing's off the table yet," Rob answered. "It might be a long shot, but it's the best lead we have right now."

"If it's all we have..." Amelia said, sounding uncertain.

"It's more than enough," Finn said, rubbing his tired eyes. "This has Vilne's style all over it. I'm sure it's him."

Amelia looked at the ground as if in disagreement for a moment. Then, she said: "It's one possibility."

Finn didn't comment, but Amelia's different perspective gnawed at him.

It has to be Vilne, he thought. *And I'm going to get him.*

"You should get moving then," Rob nodded approvingly. "You can start by visiting the crime scene. Amelia, you'll accompany Finn while I coordinate things from here. The American Embassy in London is extremely concerned about all of this. They are worried about the implications of an escaped serial killer targeting American citizens."

"Understood, Chief," Amelia replied, her expression resolute. She turned to Finn, her gaze softening. "We're going to get through this, Finn. Together. But if you feel at any time you need to pull back."

"Thanks, Amelia," Finn murmured, grateful for her unwavering support. "It's not like I'm going to fall apart. I mean, check out these guns?" He flexed his arms for a moment in jest.

Amelia rolled her eyes, but she then smiled at him.

Rob stood up and shook their hands. "Please be careful, you two."

"We will," Amelia said.

"I'd feel better if I had my gun," Finn said.

"I know," Rob replied. "But the Home Office won't approve that. If you hadn't been suspended from the FBI, they might have given you permission, but despite everything, they…"

"Don't trust me entirely," Finn said with a grin. "Well, they sure know how to make me feel at home."

"It's not that Finn, it's…" Rob started.

"Yeah, yeah," Finn said. "I get it. I burned down a hotel chasing Vilne last time in the US. They think I might be a little too reckless to go wandering around the UK with a firearm."

"For what it's worth," Rob said. "If it were my choice, we'd all be armed while this Vilne character is doing the rounds. Stay safe."

Finn nodded. "And you keep Demi safe."

"I will," Rob said. "Good luck."

As they left the office, Finn felt the weight of responsibility settling onto his shoulders once more. He knew that the trail they were about to follow could lead them deeper into danger, but it was a risk he had to take. For Demi, for Amelia and Rob, and for everyone else who might fall prey to Max Vilne's sinister games.

"Let's go, Winters," Finn said, determination replacing the fatigue in his voice. "If these two new murders are Vilne's, we're already playing catch up."

CHAPTER THREE

As Finn and Amelia pulled up to Castle Richmond, the unusual colors of the half-painted walls and turrets struck Finn as odd. The gray, white, and blue stone structure loomed over them, both imposing and baffling. Scaffolding clung to its sides like metal vines. Around its perimeter, police tape had been erected, and a couple of constables were guarding the entrance to what was still a crime scene.

Finn couldn't help but notice the outer walls, once uniformly gray, now adorned with a fresh coat of white paint, some of the turrets half-painted in pale blue.

"Looks like a kids' toy," Finn said as he opened the door and got out. Amelia soon joined him in the brisk morning air.

Above them, a gray swirl of cloud like a whirlpool hid most of the sun from the ground. Amelia stepped forward.

"It wasn't always like this, you know," Amelia said, glancing at him. "A rich American couple bought this place. They're giving it a whole new look. Up until a few months ago, it was called Hemworth Castle, and had been for hundreds of years."

Finn smirked, taking in the unconventional design choices. "May I apologize on behalf of my country."

"We have our own share of people not valuing history, believe me," Amelia said, tilting her head, studying the castle. "At least the colors are... Interesting."

"Interesting' is one way of putting it," Finn quipped. "A castle should have three things: stone, knights, and ghosts. And all of that should be spooky. It's in the rule book. Anything else is just window dressing."

"Finn, you surprise me. I didn't think you were such a stickler for tradition."

"I am the very definition of traditional," he replied, adjusting his jacket as they approached the entrance, nodding to the constables manning the perimeter.

The crisp autumn air nipped at their faces, and Finn felt the familiar stirrings of adrenaline that he always felt at the start of cases as they prepared to face the scene inside. He knew that beneath the castle's modernized exterior lay a darker truth, one that he and Amelia would have to uncover together. It was always fun, but if Vilne was around, the stakes were far higher. And Finn was still not completely recovered from the drug Vilne had used on him. He could feel it in the core of his being. He was weaker somehow.

"Ready?" Amelia asked as they approached the police tape.

"Always," Finn responded, hiding any worries about his capabilities in his current condition. "No, wait a second." Finn ran his hand through his blond hair, making sure it was sitting perfectly. "Okay, *now* I'm ready."

"Remind me to book a beauty therapist for you next time we're on a case."

As they neared the front of the castle, Finn overheard two police constables whispering animatedly. "That's them, I know it," one of them muttered, casting furtive glances in their direction. Finn couldn't help but grin, knowing that he and Amelia had gained a certain level of infamy for solving high-profile cases across the UK.

Finn winked at Amelia, who rolled her eyes and whispered, "Please don't" through gritted teeth.

"Consulting Detective, Finn Wright, at your service," Finn said in a theatrical voice to the constables. "Ably assisted by Inspector Amelia Winters."

Amelia showed her badge. "It's the other way around."

"Ah, the life of a ridiculously famous detective," Finn quipped again, his tone playful. The constables exchanged amused glances, clearly taken aback by Finn's candor.

"Are you always like this?" one asked in a strong London accent, cracking a smile.

"Only on days ending in 'y,'" Finn replied, grinning as Amelia shook her head in mock disapproval.

With a nod from the constables, Finn and Amelia stepped under the police tape and continued up to a large wooden doorway that was open.

"Do you have to embarrass us wherever we go?" Amelia asked once out of earshot.

"It's the only thing that gets me through the day," Finn said.

"I actually believe that," said Amelia.

"After you," Finn said, waving his hand towards the doorway.

Upon crossing the threshold, they were met with an unusual sight: the ancient structure boasted a modern, almost gaudy interior, a stark departure from its medieval exterior. Plush velvet furniture and gleaming metal accents stood out against worn stone walls, while abstract art adorned the towering ceilings.

"Seems like our American friends have been busy," Amelia murmured, her eyes taking in the unexpected decor.

Before Finn could respond, a season figure appeared before them: Dressed in a dark blue suit and wearing a green winter coat, the man had kind eyes and a weathered face that spoke of years spent on the force. Amelia's face lit up at the sight of him.

"Inspector Wilson!" She said, shaking his hand enthusiastically.

Finn was surprised to see Amelia so animated.

"Amelia, lovely to see you," he said from behind a thick mustache. "I've been following your recent appearances in the papers with interest."

"Inspector Wilson trained me back when I was just getting started," she explained, a note of fondness in her voice. "He's one of the best."

"Let's not get carried away, Amelia," Wilson said modestly, though the hint of a smile tugged at the corners of his mouth. "Come with me, I'll show you where we found the bodies."

"Straight to the point," Finn said. "A man after my own heart."

"Yes, Quite, Mr Wright," Inspector Wilson said. "I have enjoyed your exploits as well. Unconventional. And that's what this country needs. The unconventional. People thinking out of the box."

"Thank you," Finn replied. "And may I say you have a magnificent mustache."

Inspector Wilson looked at Finn oddly.

"Like you said, Inspector, Wilson," Amelia laughed. "Finn is a bit... Unconventional."

"This way."

As they followed Wilson through the castle's labyrinthine corridors, Finn couldn't help but marvel at the peculiar fusion of old and new that surrounded them. It was as if the very fabric of Hemworth Castle were being torn between two worlds, and in the middle, two people were dead.

The library-study, when they reached it, was a somber space cloaked in shadows. Two lifeless figures lay on the floor, their eyes still open, gazing upward at nothingness.

"This is Lily and Thomas Richmond," Inspector Wilson said, his voice heavy with the weight of the tragedy before them. "Compatriots of yours, Mr Wright. They moved here a few months ago and were in the process of turning Hemsworth into Richmond Castle."

"I doubt that work will be finished," Finn thought out loud.

Finn's gaze settled on the two bodies while Amelia observed the victims, keenly. He pulled a pair of blue forensic gloves from his pocket, snapping them on with practiced ease, and crouched down next to Lily's body, examining the fatal wound at the back of her head. "She was struck with some force," he said, looking up at Amelia and Wilson. "The skull has caved in."

"Looks like the stab wounds would have been unnecessary to get the job done," Amelia said, pointing out wounds to Lily Richmond's side. "That could imply a rage-kill or someone with a personal vendetta against her."

Wilson nodded gravely. "And Mr. Richmond here," he gestured to the man's body, "appears to have been stabbed multiple times as well. Our killer must have been incredibly confident to take on both victims simultaneously."

"Or perhaps he got lucky," Finn's eyes narrowed as he spotted a blood splatter near the door, then marched across the room to where a few scattered drops of blood caught his attention. "I think they were killed one at a time."

"Reconstruct it for us," Amelia urged, her interest piqued as she observed Finn's thought process.

"Alright," Finn said, taking a deep breath as he pieced together the sequence of events in his mind. "Thomas was attacked first—stabbed repeatedly until he succumbed to his injuries. Then Lily entered the room later, saw the body, and tried to flee. That's when the killer caught her, striking her on the back of the head with a blunt object. The killer must have been across the room as Lily had time to turn and start running, but the killer was fast."

As Finn spoke, the scene played out like a macabre film reel, the brutal violence juxtaposed against the serenity of the library. Finn could almost hear Lily's panicked footsteps echoing through the room, cut short by the sudden impact of the killer's blow.

"Confident or just insanely lucky," Amelia mused aloud. "And Look here," she continued, her voice firm as she pointed to the position of the bodies. "There is some dust on the floor, most likely from the renovations. See these streaks? Those are drag marks. The bodies must have been moved after the fact to the center of the room."

Finn nodded in agreement, his eyes scanning the room for any clues left behind by the killer.

"Placed side by side like this..." Inspector Wilson mused, furrowing his brow. "Why would the killer do that? Remorse, perhaps? Wanting them to be together in death?"

Finn shook his head slowly, his expression darkening. "I doubt it. Max Vilne is known for making a display of his victims. He didn't just kill two people; he destroyed a marriage, a union. This arrangement serves to emphasize that."

"Max Vilne?" Inspector Wilson said. "So you think it's this American fellow who escaped custody?"

"It's just a theory," Amelia said, tempering Finn's expectations. "We shouldn't prejudice ourselves in that direction yet."

Amelia's gaze lingered on the lifeless couple, as if trying to come up with a valid alternative. Finn was feeling frustrated that she wasn't on board with the Vilne hypothesis. Finn felt sure that it must be him.

"Let's consider how the murderer entered the room," Finn now said, his focus shifting as he scanned their surroundings. Moving to the back of the library, he bent down to examine something on the floor near a window. His fingers brushed over fresh flecks of paint, the same blue hue that adorned some of the castle's exterior walls.

"Inspector Wilson, you should have forensics take a close look at this window," Finn instructed, his voice steady and confident. "The killer likely climbed the scaffolding outside and came in through here."

"Some of the forensic's chaps are downstairs," Wilson said through his bushy mustache. "I'll ask them to come up."

As Wilson left to relay Finn's observations to the forensic team, Finn's eyes darted to another window in the library, this one overlooking the castle's courtyard. The light filtering in through the stained glass cast a mosaic of colors across the dusty floor, drawing his attention to the intricate patterns. He walked over, taking a moment to appreciate the craftsmanship before unlatching the window and pushing it open. The crisp autumn air rushed in, carrying with it the scent of damp earth and the faint sounds of the ongoing investigation outside.

Beneath the sill, part of the scaffolding stood.

"Oi, Finn, what are you—" Amelia's words caught in her throat as she watched him stick one leg out of the open window, perched precariously on the edge. Her protective instincts seemingly kicked in, and she took a step towards him, concern etched on her face.

"Relax, Amelia," Finn said, glancing back at her with a mischievous grin. "I'm not about to take a dive. I just want to get a better look at something."

Amelia raised an eyebrow. "And what, pray tell, is so fascinating out there that you're willing to risk life and limb for it?"

"Only one way to find out." Finn's eyes sparkled with excitement, daring her to join him. He shifted his weight, balancing effortlessly on the windowsill as he extended a hand towards her. "I'm going sightseeing. Are you coming?"

CHAPTER FOUR

The chill of the British autumn was keenly felt on the scaffolding where Finn stood, a precarious iron skeleton clinging to the ancient castle walls. His eyes, sharpened by years of attentive training, scanned the structure with a meticulous gaze. Beside him, Inspector Amelia Winters moved with a grace that belied the danger of their surroundings, though she seemed to be the more cautious of the two.

"Look at this," Amelia said, pointing to a twisted rod of metal that seemed almost gnawed upon. "It looks damaged."

Finn crouched, the cold biting through his jeans as he peered over the edge. Below, the ground lay barren of debris—a silent testament to careful planning or swift clean-up. The absence was too conspicuous, given the wreckage Finn observed.

"Amelia, I'm certain this wasn't an accident. This was the intruder's doing. He's broken a piece of scaffolding deliberately, making it look like it smashed a window over there," Finn's voice held a note of conviction, his mind piecing together fragments of the crime like a dark puzzle.

She raised an eyebrow, her silhouette stark against the backdrop of the gray late-morning sky. "Why do you say that?"

"Because," he started, pushing himself up to full height, feeling the weight of his past missteps lending gravity to his theory, "the killer didn't want this to go down as it did. He went to great lengths to hide how he came into the castle. Maybe he wanted it all to look incidental, perhaps he was going to kill the couple and make it look like an accident. Why else try to cover your tracks?"

"You think he tried to cover his tracks and botched it?" Amelia asked, sounding distant. "So let me get this straight, you're saying that the killer's initial plan was to make the broken window look like an accident rather than the work of someone breaking in?" Amelia's voice was calm yet probing, reflecting the wheels turning behind her sharp gaze.

"Exactly." Finn nodded. "But the plot went awry, didn't it? Something happened. I expect he had to come back outside when Thomas appeared unexpectedly, then Thomas either saw him out here or the killer decided to take the opportunity and came in through the nearest one. In any case, the plan went out the window, if you pardon the pun."

"Yeah, it must have," she mused aloud, tilting her head slightly. "Could Lily's unexpected presence have caused a deviation in the plan, too?"

"Lily..." Finn echoed. "Perhaps the killer wanted to break into the castle and kill Thomas in a way that looked like an accident. I bet that library study was somewhere he often sat at night, and the killer knew that. Maybe he had cased the castle out beforehand, or he had been here before. But it didn't go to plan, Thomas fought back and the killer had to resort to stabbing him. Lily's appearance forced the killer to improvise. It's messy work when plans change last minute. Then the killer moved the bodies together perhaps out of anger. He almost wanted the person who found the bodies to know that he had destroyed their lives and broke the couple apart forever. I wonder if the anger is because they didn't act the way Vilne anticipated. I could see Vilne being angry about that, he prides himself on being a mastermind."

"Possibly" Amelia's lips pressed into a thin line, her eyes scanning the expanse below.

Finn could sense that she wasn't entirely buying his line of thought. He had to admit that he wasn't firing on all cylinders. He was tired. He was still struggling physically from the drug Vilne had given him. And the stress was getting to him, despite always trying to crack a joke whenever the opportunity arose.

"Let's keep looking," she then suggested, her tone firm, yet not without a note of encouragement that seemed to beckon him back from the edge of his introspective abyss.

"Lead the way," Finn acquiesced, gesturing with an open palm. They moved in tandem across the scaffolding, which groaned under their weight, a disquieting soundtrack as Amelia hesitated and Finn now took the lead in their descent. His boots hit the soft earth with a muted thud, and he immediately noted an anomaly—the ground. Although there was no debris directly under the scaffolding, he could now see from his vantage point that the ground to the side was littered with planks of wood and a scattering of stones that seemed almost strategically placed.

"Look at this," Finn called up to Amelia, who was a few rungs above him on the ladder. He knelt beside the debris, his fingers running over the rough texture of a wooden shard. "Not just random fallout from the construction."

Amelia joined him on the ground, her gaze sharp as she surveyed the scene. "The killer placed them here?" Her voice carried a note of skepticism mingled with intrigue.

"Too clean for a collapse," Finn replied, standing and gesturing toward the untouched mud around them. "Whoever came through here didn't want to leave tracks."

"Precautions," Amelia murmured, nodding slowly. "This killer thinks steps ahead. They knew we'd look for prints. We shouldn't walk on that piece of ground in case there is a trace. Let forensics do their thing. But it does look like the killer has hidden any marks." She paced the perimeter, her mind visibly sifting through scenarios.

"Exactly," Finn said, feeling the familiar rush of adrenaline when pieces began to align. "He covered his trail, but he can't cover everything. Not forever."

"Should we go further out from here?" Amelia suggested, her eyes already scouting the treeline beyond. "There might be more to find beyond the immediate scene."

"Agreed." Finn clung to the side of the castle for the moment and checked the stability of his footing on some brickwork that jutted out before they proceeded. Once far enough from the scene, he made his way over the frozen ground. The desolate frozen grass soon gave way to dense bushes and marshy terrain, the air thick with the scent of wet foliage and earth. As they pushed through the greenery, the squelch of mud beneath their boots betrayed the sodden nature of their path.

"Careful now, Amelia," Finn said, half-joking, "if you fall and get stuck, I might have to use you as a bridge."

"There would be another murder if that happened," Amelia retorted with a wry smile. "Let's fan out a bit," Amelia instructed, her eyes scanning the uneven terrain. "We'll cover more ground that way."

"Copy that," Finn replied, taking a parallel path to Amelia's as they continued their search. With each step, he felt the urgency of their investigation pressing upon him—time was slipping away, and with it, the killer's trail grew colder.

Amelia paused, her boot resting on a firmer patch of earth that seemed out of place amid the squelching morass. She crouched down, brushing aside a cluster of wet leaves with a forensic delicacy that Finn admired despite the urgency clawing at his insides.

"Look at this," she said, her voice low and steady. "Ground's been disturbed here, but not like the rest. It's too... even."

Finn joined her, his knees sinking slightly into the cold ground as he examined what she had uncovered: a narrow path, the undergrowth trampled in a way that suggested careful, repeated passage.

"Someone's been using this," Finn murmured, his eyes tracing the line of the trail as it weaved through the thicket. His pulse quickened—not from fear, but from the thrill of the chase. This was a tangible clue, a thread they could pull.

"Whoever it is might have left more than just a trail," Amelia replied, already moving forward with purpose. "Let's see where this leads."

Their footsteps were soft on the compacted earth, senses heightened as they advanced now through woodland. The canopy above filtered the light into a cool, dappled pattern that played tricks on the eyes. Finn took in every rustle, every bird's call that sliced through the stillness, cataloging potential threats.

"Watch your step," Amelia cautioned as they approached a break in the foliage. "There's something up ahead."

The trail opened onto a small clearing, and there, cutting across the muddy terrain, were the unmistakable impressions of tire tracks—deep and defined, recent enough to have avoided being washed away by the elements.

"It must be those green eyes," Finn said. "You picked that up quickly." A vehicle in this remote location was no coincidence; it was a lead, one that connected the castle to the outside world, to an escape route.

"It's a super power," Amelia joked as she took some photos on her phone of the tire tracks. "Forensics will have a field day with these," she commented, pocketing the camera once she was satisfied with the shots. "Tyre treads can tell us make and model, maybe even point us to a specific vehicle if we're lucky."

"Or at least confirm someone had reason to hide their visit," Finn added. He stood beside Amelia, surveying the tracks that disappeared back into the woods. "These look like the type of tracks an SUV would leave. It might tie into my theory that the killer cased the castle first and chose their point of entry carefully. Maybe he visited here more than once. If it is Vilne, he is meticulous."

"Let's get these measured," Amelia said, determination sharpening her features. "It's at least a lead of sorts."

A mist was slowly forming on the cold air like a prowling animal, creeping along the castle's ancient stones as Finn cast his gaze towards its towering silhouette. "We should head back," he said, his voice cutting through the damp air with the decisiveness of a man who had learned to trust his instincts above all else.

"Back inside?" Amelia asked. Her eyes were still fixed on the tire tracks that dwindled into the forest, but her stance suggested readiness for whatever came next.

"We should leave the rest to forensics in case we contaminate the scene. There's a lot of mud around here. Besides, whoever found the bodies might have seen something they didn't realize was important," Finn explained, turning on his heel and leading the way through the thicket they'd emerged from.

"True," Amelia conceded, following close behind. They wove between the trees, the branches snagging at their clothes like desperate hands trying to pull them back. The sound of their passage disturbed birds perched in the hidden alcoves among the leaves, sending them fluttering skyward in a fluster of wings.

"And I want to know if Max Vilne killed Thomas Richmond," Finn said. "To cover his tracks into the country."

Amelia said nothing, and Finn could feel her skepticism as they approached the castle walls.

CHAPTER FIVE

The air within the castle's stone walls was warmer than outside, to Finn at least. But an icy draft that felt musty could be felt, fighting against that warmth, an ancient chill that seemed to cling to the crevices of the mottled gray blocks. Finn could feel the weight of what had happened there during the night pressing against him as he and Amelia Winters crossed the threshold, their footsteps resounding with a hollow echo in the grand entrance hall.

"Inspector Wright, Detective Winters," came a crisp voice from the shadow of the grand staircase. Inspector Wilson emerged, the lines on his face drawn tight, some of them disappearing beneath his thick, graying mustache.

"Wilson," Finn acknowledged with a nod, his gaze scanning the vast space, as if expecting the secrets of the castle to leap from the ornate cornices.

"The bodies have been taken away," Wilson said, clasping his hands behind his back. "They're en route to the morgue. Autopsy scheduled immediately, though we may still have a bit of a wait."

"Any preliminary findings during the initial investigation to add to what we already know?" Amelia asked, her voice betraying nothing of the unease that such grandeur mixed with death often stirred.

"Nothing conclusive yet. It's..." Wilson paused, searching for the right words, "...messy."

Finn's jaw tightened. He had seen 'messy' before, the kind of chaotic aftermath that told stories of struggle and desperation.

"Seems this place has seen its fair share of history. Now it's got a bit more," Finn said, eyes lingering on a portrait - one of only a few left on the walls - where past owners of a long-gone era looked down with austere disapproval.

"Indeed," Wilson replied. "Any luck outside?"

Amelia stepped beside Finn, her gaze following his. "We think we found some tracks outside leading to woodland, and then some impressions that look like someone drove a car back there."

"And I bet they weren't sightseeing," Finn muttered, turning back to Wilson.

"I'll have someone take care of that for you," Wilson interjected, "I wonder if the killer acted alone."

"Vilne manipulates," Finn said. "He gets people to do some of his dirty work through blackmail and other means, but when it comes to the actual killing, he does that himself. That's the part he lives for."

"If it was him," Amelia said firmly. "We need to keep our minds open."

Finn sighed.

"Understood," Wilson acknowledged with respect in his tone. "Is there anything else you need from me here?"

"We were wanting to talk with whoever found the bodies," Finn said, putting aside his mild annoyance that Amelia kept fighting his theory about Vilne.

"Not a problem," Wilson said. "It was the caretaker. Let me introduce you to him, he's still here."

"Lead on, Sir," Amelia said, then blushing.

"You're in charge here, Amelia," Wilson smiled, kindly.

"Sorry, force of habit," Amelia said, continuing on.

"You never call *me* Sir," Finn said, walking alongside her.

"You'd have to be a gentleman, first," Amelia answered.

"I'll have you know I am down with the etiquette," Finn said, opening a door and holding it for Amelia. "Hah! See?"

"There's more to being a gentleman than holding doors open," Amelia laughed. "Besides, I like to open them for myself. It is the 21st century."

Wilson let out a loud laugh. "Haven't changed a bit, Amelia. Give them hell, and don't let them forget it."

"She gives me hell every day," Finn replied.

"And would you have it any other way?" Amelia asked as they rounded a corner.

Finn didn't answer. He just smiled at her. No, he wouldn't have had it any other way.

"Through these doors," Wilson now added, the joviality now replaced by a clear tone of professionalism.

They walked through a large archway and entered a large hall that hadn't been renovated yet. It had all of the charm of an ancestral castle, with swords on the walls, tapestries, and a huge mantel fireplace. The hall no doubt long ago was resplendent with echoes of laughter and clinking glasses, had grown hushed, its ancient stone absorbing the day's grim addition to its history. As Finn and Amelia traversed the threshold, a figure detached himself from the shadows near a tapestry that told tales of battles long since won and lost.

"Inspector Winters, Mr. Wright, this is Mr. Parker," Inspector Wilson said, gesturing towards the caretaker—a man whose face was drawn tight, eyes sunken as though he had seen something terrible and couldn't remove it from his mind.

"He's been quite cooperative," Wilson added.

"Mr. Parker." Finn nodded, extending a hand that the other man took reluctantly, his grip weak, tremulous.

"Sir," Mr. Parker managed, faltering under the scrutiny of their gazes. Amelia noted the pallor of his skin, the way his hands couldn't find rest, fluttering like caged birds at his sides.

"Could you tell us how well you knew the deceased?" Finn inquired, his tone careful not to pry too harshly into the caretaker's fragile state.

"Not—uh—not very well, I'm afraid." Mr. Parker swallowed hard, his Adam's apple bobbing awkwardly. "I was kept on by the previous owners, see. The Harringtons. Been here for over thirty years, but the new owners—" His voice cracked, betraying him.

"Did they keep much contact with you? Did you see them often?" Amelia asked, stepping closer. She watched as Mr. Parker's gaze dipped to the floor, fixating on an invisible point between the flagstones.

"Only when necessary," he muttered. "They had their own... way of doing things, separate from how it's always been done here."

"Change can be difficult," Finn offered, his tone neither accusatory nor dismissive as he studied Mr. Parker. The man was a reed in the wind, Finn thought, bending to whichever force was strongest at the time.

"Very difficult," Mr. Parker echoed, voice barely above a whisper.

Finn glanced at Amelia, sharing a silent communication. They were both thinking it: Mr. Parker was more than just a nervous bystander. But what he was exactly remained to be seen.

"Thank you, Mr. Parker," Amelia said gently. "You've been through a shock. How did you find Lily and Thomas?"

"I live in a nearby village, so I usually come up first thing in the morning around 6AM," the man said, mournfully. "I found them in the library... Well, it was a library, I think Mr Richmond was having it turned into some sort of den."

Finn observed the man's disdain.

"You clearly didn't like their approach to the castle?" Finn asked.

"Mrs Richmond was fine," he said. "She wanted to keep the castle as it had always been."

"How do you know that?" Amelia asked.

"The castle echoes," he answered. "It's hard to keep secrets if you don't keep your voice down."

There was quiet for a moment, and in that quiet, Finn studied the man.

"What is it?" Mr Parker asked, responding to Finn's stare.

Amelia's voice cut through the tension like a scalpel, clinical yet not unkind. "Mr. Parker, can you think of anyone who might have wished harm upon Lily and Thomas?"

The caretaker's eyes darted from the polished floor to the grand portraits that lined the walls, as if seeking counsel from the faces of long-dead lords and ladies. His discomfort was palpable. Finn's gaze narrowed slightly, picking up on the nuance of every shift in Mr. Parker's stance.

"Resentment," Mr. Parker finally murmured, the word hanging awkwardly in the air between them. "There was...resentment in the village and surrounding towns. Not everyone was pleased with Americans owning this place."

"Resentment strong enough to lead to murder?" Finn probed, his mind already sifting through possible motives and suspects. The fact that Lily and Thomas weren't embraced by the community could be an understated way of suggesting deeper hostility.

Mr. Parker seemed momentarily lost in thought, then gave a small shake of his head as though to clear it. "It's complicated," he said, his hands twisting together in a display of nervous energy.

Amelia stepped forward, her presence commanding yet comforting. "And the renovations? They were quite extensive, from what we've seen. Did that contribute to the ill will?"

"Ah, yes." A tight nod from Mr. Parker accompanied his words. "Didn't sit well with most folks hereabouts. Times change, but some things..." He trailed off, looking wistfully at a tapestry depicting a mythic hunt. "Some things should remain untouched."

"Did it bother you?" Finn watched the man closely.

"Me? At first. But a man's got to eat. Lily had a way about her. Couldn't help but like her." Mr. Parker's lips twitched into a brief semblance of a smile. "Thomas, though..." His face closed off again as quickly as it had opened. "He didn't understand the castle. Not really. It wasn't just a project to us—the castle is a symbol of the community."

"What is it about the castle that is so special to the people here?" Finn asked. He understood that an old castle had historical importance, but as Parker spoke, it seemed that there was more to it than that.

Parker's eyes lit up. "Have you heard of King Arthur?"

Finn looked at Amelia with a hint of excitement. "As in the mythical king of the Britons?"

"Well," Parker said. "It depends who you ask, but we believe he was Celtic, and the Cornish people have their roots in that same culture. The castle is said to be built on Arthur's grave."

"There are several places that lay claim to that," Amelia added. "We don't even know if he existed or if he was just a symbol."

"He was a symbol," Parker continued. "And legend says that when the British Isles are at their darkest moment, about to fall to an outside enemy, that Arthur will rise up to protect us all."

Finn loved such stories, though he couldn't put much stock in them. However, he understood why others would. "So that's why the castle is so important, it's supposed to be King Arthur's resting place until he is needed again?"

"Look," Parker said. "I'm not saying I believe all that, just that some do. Even if you don't believe in the idea that Arthur will return—most wouldn't these days—there are so many stories in our folklore that even some academics think that a king was buried here, and that he was the inspiration behind the legend of King Arthur."

"Is there anything else that makes the castle important?" Amelia asked.

Parker nodded. "Take your pick from history. It was a beacon of hope for people, holding out against any invaders. And it was used during World War II as a place of research for figuring out German codes. That helped us win the war and keep everyone safe. Then, there's the previous owners, all of them had a tradition of opening the castle up to the community, hosting events and gatherings. Thomas Richmond put an end to that. He said he would open the place up again when renovations were completed, but his ideas were deeply frowned upon. Some would say, offensive."

"So for Thomas, perhaps sometimes the heart must adapt, or risk..." Amelia began, but then paused, choosing her words carefully, "...stagnation."

"Perhaps," Mr. Parker conceded. "But you can also buy something you don't understand. Why buy a castle if you are going to turn it into something else?"

The stony silence of the castle's grand hall was punctuated only by the subtle crackle of the hearth as Finn turned his inquisitive gaze back to Mr. Parker, a furrow of concern etched across his brow. The caretaker seemed diminished somehow, smaller against the vast tapestries that draped the walls, depicting battles long since faded into legend.

"Mr. Parker," Finn began, his voice steady and probing, "was there anyone in particular who took the renovations harder than others? Someone who might have been... vocally opposed?"

"No, not really," Mr. Parker replied, shaking his head, the movement sending a ripple through the thinning strands of his hair. "Just a general annoyance, you understand? It's hard to point fingers when it's the air that's thick with disapproval."

Amelia stepped closer, her shadow merging with Finn's upon the cold stone floor. "Has anything unusual happened recently? Anything out of the ordinary that might help us understand what went on here?"

"Two days ago," Mr. Parker started, hesitantly, "I saw someone. He was taking pictures of the grounds. I chased him off but didn't get a good look at his face." He wrung his hands, the skin reddened from years of labor. "Tall man, dark hair—that's all I remember."

Finn exchanged a knowing glance with Amelia, the corners of his eyes tightening. Max Vilne was tall, dark-haired, and had an uncanny ability to be both present and invisible. Could he be lurking so close, orchestrating chaos once again?

"Was that out by the woods out front?" Finn asked.

"Yes," Mr Parker replied sounding surprised. "How do you know that?"

"We found something there," Finn said, not wanting to commit any other information.

"Thank you, Mr. Parker," Amelia said softly, her hand briefly touching the caretaker's arm in a gesture of comfort. "You've been very helpful."

As they moved away, each step felt like a descent into a deeper enigma, the castle's oppressive atmosphere clinging to them as if loath to let go. Finn's mind raced, piecing together fragments of information, the image of a tall, dark-haired figure behind the lens of a camera slowly sharpening into focus. Max Vilne's specter seemed to stretch across the countryside, and Finn could feel the net of the killer's game drawing tighter around them.

Mr Parker looked forlorn and turned to stare at the fire. "I didn't like what the Richmonds were doing. But no one deserves... That..."

He put his head in his hands as though trying to wipe away the image of seeing both murdered bodies.

"Your assistance has been invaluable, Mr. Parker," Finn said, extending a firm handshake to the shaken caretaker whose eyes still echoed the horror of his gruesome discovery. "It can be hard seeing what you did."

"We can get you referred for some counseling through your GP if you like?" Amelia offered, softly.

"No... No, I'll be fine."

"Again, thank you," Finn said, feeling sorry for the man.

"Anything to help get to the bottom of this dreadful business," Mr. Parker replied, giving a slight nod as he accepted Finn and Amelia's wordless expression of thanks—a subtle tilt of Amelia's head acknowledging the weight the man carried as the bearer of bad news.

"I'll stay here and finish up on a few things," Wilson offered. "If you need anything from me, let me know."

"Thanks, Wilson," Finn said.

"I hope to see you soon under better circumstances," Amelia added.

As they turned to leave, Finn's phone vibrated abruptly against his thigh, a sudden intrusion that made him pause mid-stride. He glanced at the screen—Rob's name flashed urgently.

"Rob?" Finn's voice was crisp, cutting through the hush that had settled in the corridor.

"Finn... Bad news. Someone's had a crack at my aunt's cottage in Great Amwell," came the blunt reply, Rob's concern barely masked by his gruff tone. "Whoever did it, must have known you've been staying there. They've done a number on one of the windows and unlocked the door from the inside when they were leaving, but it's odd—nothing appears to be touched inside as far as we can tell."

Finn thought for a moment, feeling dread creeping in. Vilne knew where he lived now. That was dangerous. "He's unlocked the door so we know someone went inside, otherwise it's just a broken window... Vilne... He's done this for a reason."

"Considering you are already in the area," Rob advised. "And it's possible Vilne murdered the Richmonds, I think it would be good for you to come by and see what you make of the break in."

"Thanks, Rob. We're on our way there now... And... Keep looking over your shoulder, Vilne could be after you, too." Finn ended the call, and without needing to articulate it, Amelia said "we better go".

33

As Finn and Amelia left the grand hall behind, Finn wondered if anywhere would be safe for him and his friends.

CHAPTER SIX

Finn's mind was full of unanswered questions as he drove towards Great Amwell. The gentle hum of the engine and the rhythmic swipe of the windshield wipers set a steady cadence as Finn maneuvered the car through the damp British countryside. Droplets of icy rain clung to the windows, distorting the yellowed pastures and hedgerows that blurred past them. Amelia sat in the passenger seat, her gaze fixed on the passing scenery, her fingers tapping an absent-minded rhythm on her knee.

"Have you heard from Demi lately?" Amelia's voice cut through the quiet interior of the car, as unexpected as a siren on an empty road.

Finn glanced over, his grip tightening on the steering wheel. "We've been in touch for the last few weeks ever since she came to the UK," he said, his words measured. "She's... *It's* complicated."

Amelia nodded, her eyes never leaving the window. "I can only imagine."

A heavy silence settled between them. Finn thought back to their previous case when Amelia and he had kissed while facing almost certain death. The kiss they had shared—a moment of vulnerability amid chaos—loomed in Finn's mind like an unspoken promise. It was a ghost that lingered at the edge of their partnership, ethereal and untouchable. Finn still wondered what it had meant and whether he should speak about it at all.

"About that night—" Finn suddenly began, his voice barely above the whisper of tires on wet asphalt.

"Let's not," Amelia interjected, her tone firm but gentle. She finally turned to look at him, her green eyes holding his for a fleeting second. "Things are complicated for you right now, and we got lost in the moment. It happens. We should forget it."

"Right." Finn's response was automatic, but inside, a sharp pang of disappointment twisted. He felt crushed, as if the possibility of something incredible had slipped through his fingers, irretrievable. He wasn't sure whether he wanted to get back together with Demi or start something new with Amelia. He cared deeply for both, but he had to admit that in his mind, Demi was fading, their connection broken by her leaving him. She claimed that someone had blackmailed her to leave him, but even if that were true, he had come to realize that their relationship had been on sinking ground for some time.

Above all else, he didn't want to hurt either Amelia or Demi, and if the best option to ensure that meant being alone, maybe he had to consider that, too.

He shook the thoughts and focused on the road ahead, the steady thrum of the engine a metronome to his scattered desires. The windshield wipers continued their back-and-forth dance, each swipe an attempt to clear away more than just rain.

The quaint village of Great Amwell had a deceptive calm about it, as if the rolling green and yellow hills and cobblestone paths dusted with frost were untouched by time or turmoil. Finn's car rolled to a stop outside the cottage, its thatched roof heavy with the weight of recent rain. He turned off the ignition, and both he and Amelia sat for a moment, taking in the scene.

"Looks peaceful enough," Amelia said, breaking the silence as she unclasped her seat belt. "Although you've been living here for months now, I'm surprised they haven't tried to have you evicted."

"I'll have you know I am a model neighbor," Finn replied.

"Still, it is a serene place," Amelia continued.

"Appearances can be deceiving," Finn replied, his eyes scanning the perimeter with practiced vigilance before stepping out of the car.

As they approached, Rob emerged from the front door. His face was grim, etched with concern. "This isn't good, Finn," he said without any pleasantries. "You shouldn't be staying here anymore. It's not safe. If you had been here..."

Finn met Rob's gaze squarely. "If Vilne wants to find me, I'd rather it be here than anywhere else," he asserted, his voice carrying the undertone of a man who had seen too much yet refused to back down. "I need to end this. If he comes to me, all the better. I'll prepare for it."

"Stubborn as ever," Rob muttered, but there was no real heat in his words. They all understood what was at stake.

They stepped inside, the warmth of the interior doing little to dispel the chill that had nothing to do with the weather. Finn took in the familiar space, now tainted with the violation of his privacy. There was a tense energy in the air, like the electric buzz before lightning struck.

"Max Vilne is playing with you," Amelia observed, her hand hovering over the back of a chair as if touching something fragile. "He's taunting you, pulling you into his game."

"Then let's not disappoint him." Finn's jaw clenched, his mind racing through scenarios, each one more treacherous than the last.

"Look, mate," Rob began, clapping a hand on Finn's shoulder, a gesture of solidarity. "We're in this together. But you shouldn't bring any unnecessary heat. You've got to think about the others—about Amelia."

"Do you think I'd ever want to put Amelia in danger?" Finn shot back, but there was a flicker of doubt in his eyes, a brief hesitation that betrayed his deeper fears.

"Boys, I can take care of myself," Amelia interjected, her tone laced with both annoyance and assurance. "But Finn, if Vilne is targeting the places you frequent..."

"Then I'll make sure this ends with me before he gets to anyone else," Finn interrupted, his resolve hardening. Inside, though, a tumultuous sea of concern threatened to drown him. This wasn't just about him anymore; the people he cared about were in Vilne's line of sight. And that was something he couldn't bear.

"Max Vilne doesn't play by the rules," Rob said, his voice low. "You know that better than anyone."

"Which is why we have to be two steps ahead," Finn replied, his eyes narrowing as he scanned the room, every sense attuned to the unseen dangers that might still linger within these walls.

The three of them stood there, a trio bound by duty and the unspoken acknowledgment that whatever came next would test them in ways they couldn't yet foresee.

The cottage door creaked on its hinges, an ominous welcome that seemed to mock their intrusion. Stale air greeted them as they entered, the kind of silence that suffocated. Finn's gaze swept across the sitting room, his mind cataloging the placement of every cushion, the angle of each chair.

"Everything's just as I left it," Rob muttered, brows knotted in confusion. "Why break in and not take anything? It doesn't make sense."

"Vilne never does anything without reason," Finn replied. His voice was steady, but inside, his thoughts churned like a stormy sea. He moved through the house methodically, eyes darting to corners, seeking the anomaly he knew must be there.

"Could just be intimidation, right?" Amelia's asked.

"Maybe. But that's an appetizer for Vilne." Finn approached the staircase, his footsteps muffled by the thick carpet. As he ascended, his ears strained for the sound of something amiss—the whisper of displaced air, the faintest scent of intruder. Nothing.

"Check the kitchen, Rob," Finn called over his shoulder before striding into the main bedroom. The bed, neatly made, looked undisturbed. Sunlight filtered through the curtains, casting a warm glow that belied the cold knot in Finn's gut.

He reached the bedside and hesitated, a moment suspended in time. Then, with deliberate slowness, he lifted the pillow. There, nestled beneath, were three small figures—dolls, eerily precise in their detail.

"Amelia, Rob—up here," Finn's call was calm, but his pulse thrummed against his skin, adrenaline infusing his veins.

They gathered around him, and he held the dolls out for inspection, his fingers careful not to disturb them more than necessary. Each one was meticulously crafted, with features that bore a striking resemblance to those present—and one conspicuously absent.

"Damn it," Amelia breathed out, her eyes flicking from the dolls to Finn. "You were right. He's sending a message."

"Seems like it," Finn conceded, his jaw set. These weren't mere toys; they were messages, threats woven in thread and porcelain.

"Let's bag these up," Amelia said, her professionalism masking the unease that flickered in her gaze. "Forensics might find something we can use."

"Right." Finn nodded, though part of him wanted to fling the dolls into the fireplace, watch them melt away into nothingness. But he couldn't; they were evidence now, a tangible link to the twisted mind they were up against.

"Be thorough," he instructed, his eyes lingering on the dolls a moment longer before he turned away, already plotting their next move in this deadly game of cat and mouse.

The tableau before them was one of mock captivity: three small figures, each bound and gagged with meticulous care. One wore the unmistakable garb of British police, while another boasted fiery red locks, and the third, a mane as black as a raven's wing. The precision unnerved Finn; it was an invasion not just of his space but of their lives.

"Rob, Amelia, Demi," Finn stated, his voice carrying a weight that seemed to press upon the room's already thick atmosphere. He pointed to each doll in turn, the connection undeniable.

"Christ," Rob muttered, rubbing the back of his neck, his gaze fixed on the miniature effigies with a mix of anger and disbelief.

"This seems like a follow-up to the note he left at the hotel," Amelia noted sharply, her eyes narrowing as she reached for a pair of evidence gloves from her coat pocket. "He wants us to know who he's targeting, so he can make you feel powerless, Finn, if you fail."

Finn felt the pressure of responsibility bear down on him. "I'm sorry—this..." He gestured vaguely at the scene, words momentarily escaping him. "It's because of me that he's dragged you all into this."

"Stop that," Amelia cut in briskly, slipping on the gloves with practiced ease. "We knew what we were signing up for being part of this. Besides, I'm not some damsel in distress," she added with a half-smile that didn't quite reach her eyes.

"Still, maybe I should step away from the team." Finn's suggestion hung heavy between them, a specter of retreat. "Keep the danger to myself."

"Cut the martyr act, Finn." Amelia's tone was gentle but firm. "You're our partner. That means we stick together, no matter how ugly it gets. Do you know how insufferable you would be if you took all this on your own? We'd never hear the end of it."

She smiled then reached out, her hands deft as they began to collect the dolls. Carefully, she placed each one into individual evidence bags, sealing them with a precision that spoke of countless hours spent preserving crime scenes.

"Let's get these to forensics," she said, her focus absolute. "Every clue gets us closer to stopping him."

As she worked, Finn watched her, admiration mingling with concern. She was right, of course—about partnership, about strength in unity—but the gnawing fear for their safety refused to be silenced.

"Rob, can I have a word?" Finn said, moving out of the house.

The garden was a quiet sanctuary compared to the chaos of the investigation. Overgrown ivy stems clung to the stone walls, having long since lost their leaves, and the air carried the scent of damp earth and decay. Finn watched a solitary red-breasted robin bob through the air, its song a soft background drone.

"He seems happy," Rob said, pointing to the bird.

"Winter has come," Finn said. "It's going to be tough for him."

There was another silence before anyone spoke.

"Is this about Demi?" Rob asked as a breeze floated by.

"What do you mean?" Finn asked.

"I'm assuming you want her sent back home," he explained.

Finn had thought about that, but there was a deep conflict within him. Part of him felt that if he sent her back to the US, that would truly be the end of them, and he wasn't certain if that was how he wanted things to pan out. But he knew even if he wanted her to go, she would try and stay. She said she wasn't going to leave unless it was with him.

"I'd rather she be here," Finn concluded out loud. "She can be under protection here, and I can keep an eye on her while Vilne is still on the loose. Back home, I can't do that. She would be exposed to his attacks, I have no doubt he'd hire or manipulate others into harming her."

Finn glanced over his shoulder, making certain that Amelia wasn't within earshot.

"Rob, listen to me," Finn said, his voice low, his gaze tracing the path of the bird as it flew over a fence. "Amelia—she's got guts, no one's denying that. But she needs to be off this case for her own sake."

Rob crossed his arms, his face set in the stubborn lines that Finn knew all too well. "You don't give her enough credit. She's the most capable Inspector I know. We need her, Finn. Her intuition, her skills—they're irreplaceable."

"Doesn't matter how capable she is if she ends up like those dolls upstairs," Finn muttered, his hand raking through his hair in frustration. The memory of the three figures, bound and gagged, was branded into his mind's eye.

"Your concern is admirable, but misplaced," Rob shot back, his voice rising slightly before he checked himself. "I won't sideline her. She'd fight it all the way, and we need our best on this."

Finn turned to face him fully, his eyes meeting Rob's in a silent plea. "And what about you? You think you're not at risk here?" he asked, the protective instinct flaring within him, a flame that refused to be snuffed out.

"Risk comes with the job," Rob replied, steadfast as ever. Then, softer, "Remember college back in the States? When my dad passed, and everything seemed to crumble? I was ready to throw it all away—to drop out."

Finn nodded, the recollection bittersweet. He had been there, pulling Rob back from the edge of despair, anchoring him when the currents of grief threatened to drag him under.

"You saved me, Finn. You kept me in the game," Rob continued, his eyes holding a depth of gratitude that words could scarce convey. "Let me repay the favor. Let me stand with you now."

Before Finn could respond, the back door creaked open, halting their conversation. Amelia stepped out, phone still pressed to her ear, her expression a carefully composed mask that did little to hide the urgency sparking in her eyes.

"Sorry to interrupt," she said, pocketing her phone, "but that was the pathologist. There's something off about the autopsies on Thomas and Lily. It's...strange. We need to go."

"Strange how?" Finn asked, the detective in him instantly alert, his thoughts pivoting to the new mystery at hand.

"Didn't say over the phone. Only that we should see for ourselves." Amelia's brow furrowed, her lips pressed in a thin line of determination.

"Then we're wasting time." Finn's voice was decisive, the unease momentarily shelved. They had a new lead, and every second counted.

CHAPTER SEVEN

Finn smelled the sterile scent of antiseptic mingled with a cold draft as he and Amelia stepped into the morgue, his former Special Agent training kicking in as he surveyed the room. Stainless steel and white tiles reflected the harsh lighting above, creating an atmosphere that was both clinical and unforgiving.

Hemworth hospital's morgue was serving as their temporary base of operations, a mere stone's throw from Richmond castle, still a crime scene.

"Inspector Winters," a man in his fifties with a balding head, beady eyes, and a white lab coat on, greeted, nodding towards Amelia who stopped and stood by a gurney, her posture rigid but her eyes revealing a storm of thoughts beneath a calm exterior.

"Agent Wright, I presume?" the man then said, acknowledging him with a curt nod. "I'm Dr. Henley, shall we go over the preliminary findings for Lily and Thomas Richmond? I think you'll find it quite thrilling."

"I don't find people being dead, thrilling, Doc," Finn said.

"Of course," the man retorted. "What I mean is the chase."

"Right, let's hear it then, Doctor," Finn said, folding his arms across his chest, trying to shake off the chill that had nothing to do with the room's temperature.

Dr. Henley, a man whose features were as sharp as the scalpels he wielded, peered at them through round spectacles. He gestured towards an array of photographs spread out on a nearby table. "Our murder weapon," he began, pointing at an X-ray image, "we believe is a medieval dirk, or something quite similar in design."

"Medieval?" Finn echoed, leaning forward to inspect the images more closely. The outline of the deep incision was unmistakable, even amid the shadows of tissue and bone, but it looked like many others Finn had seen before. He was unsure of Henley's conclusion.

"Indeed," Dr. Henley confirmed.

"How can you be sure it wasn't an ordinary knife?" Finn asked.

"The shape of the wound and some oxidized metal on the bone," Henley continued. "I've never seen it, but I was able to compare the shape and samples to a similar case in Romania where an ancient dagger was used in a murder case."

"That's... Different," Amelia observed.

"Not your typical choice for a murder weapon in this day and age, eh? In fact, this is a first for me. The idea that a weapon not used for hundreds of years has been wielded once more, it's poetic... And tragic, of course." The doctor seemed to add that in at the last moment.

Amelia picked up one of the photos, her fingers tracing the shape of the weapon as if she could feel its weight. "So we're looking for an antique? Possibly someone with access to historical artifacts?"

"Or a very dedicated murderer," Finn added, his mind racing through possibilities, motives.

"I wonder if it's from the castle," Amelia added. "There were plenty of old swords on the walls. The killer could have opportunistically grabbed one and used it to kill Thomas and Lily."

"Lily Richmond looks to have died from blunt force trauma to the back of the head," Dr. Henley interjected.

"But the stab wounds?" Finn asked.

"Superficial," Henley replied. "They could have been done afterwards, it wouldn't be the first time a

killer has mutilated a body."

"Or to make sure she was dead," Amelia replied.

"Antique swords..." Finn mused. He recalled the disgruntlement of locals over the castle's renovations. Was it possible the killer had chosen such an anachronistic tool as a statement?

Finn stood over the stainless steel slab, where the coroner had meticulously arranged photographs of the wounds for analysis. The chill of the morgue seemed to seep into his thoughts, crystallizing them with a surgeon's precision.

"Note the trajectory," the coroner said, pointing to a series of gruesome close-ups. "Lily Richmond's wounds look to have been inflicted after she was hit on the head and had died. But Thomas... Some of his were during the active attack, and of those, each entry wound is low on the body, suggesting the assailant struck from a position of lesser height."

"Or they could have been kneeling," Finn countered softly, but he knew the angles told a more telling story.

"Unlikely," Amelia interjected, leaning closer to the images. Her voice carried an analytical edge. "These are upward thrusts with considerable force. It suggests someone short, perhaps even diminutive in stature." She glanced at Finn, her eyes reflecting the sterile light fixtures above.

"Exactly my thought," the coroner agreed, tapping the photograph. "I would say it's possible the killer is a woman."

Finn let out a sigh. If that were the case, then it wouldn't have been Vilne. Max Vilne stood even taller than Finn. But then, he wouldn't put it past him to fake the trajectory.

"Let's consider the weapon," Amelia proposed, turning back to the coroner. "We're dealing with something medieval, a dirk. It's not your everyday choice for murder."

"Could it have been taken from the castle?" Finn asked, his brow furrowing as he considered the implications.

"Stolen, you mean?" The coroner shook his head. "We've checked the inventory. Nothing seems amiss, but that doesn't rule out the possibility of a private collection."

"Replicas are common enough," Finn muttered, pacing slowly.

"True," Amelia conceded. "But to choose such a distinctive weapon—it's theatrical, almost like the killer wanted it to be found, to send a message."

"Or to mislead us," Finn suggested, his mind crafting and discarding theories with each step. "The question is, to what end?" His gaze returned to the photographs, his mind constructing the profile of their suspect. Short, precise, and with a penchant for the dramatic—a killer cloaked in the shadows of the past.

Finn's fingers traced the edge of the stainless steel autopsy table, his eyes narrowing in thought. A chill from the morgue's climate-controlled air brushed against his skin, but it was the chill of realization that held him still.

"Amelia," Finn started, his voice carrying a new weight. "The locals have been quite vocal about their discontent with the castle renovations. Lily and Thomas were transforming something ancient into something modern. It's possible that our killer is making a statement with this—this medieval dirk."

"Isn't it a listed building?" Dr. Henley inquired.

"Listed?" Finn asked.

"Yes," Amelia said. "Many buildings are listed, which means it's illegal to alter them because they are historical artifacts in of themselves. But I remember reading about the works a few weeks ago and one of the reasons people were so angry, was because they were given permission to do the alterations, mainly because of some legal loophole."

"I still think the fact that an old blade was used..." Finn trailed off.

"Symbolism?" Amelia leaned back against the cold wall, her arms folded as she considered the angle. "Murder as a form of protest?"

"Exactly," Finn affirmed, stepping closer to the photographs pinned on the board. The sharp lines of the victims' wounds stood out grimly. "It's as if they wanted to use the past itself as a weapon against progress."

"An act of defiance." Amelia's gaze followed Finn's. "But it's one thing to disagree with change, another to kill for it."

"Desperate people do desperate things," Finn said, his thoughts racing. He could almost see the shadowy figure moving through the castle, the glint of the blade a silent echo of the past.

"Then we're looking for someone who not only resents the castle's new life but understands its history well enough to turn it lethal." Amelia's words were clipped, tinged with a mix of intrigue and apprehension.

"Someone steeped in the traditions... Someone local..." Finn replied, the pieces clicking together in his mind like the tumblers of a lock. "And we need to find them before..."

Before either could delve further into theories, a sudden clamor erupted from beyond the morgue's heavy door, slicing through the quiet like the dirk itself.

"What on earth—" Amelia began, her detective instincts kicking in as the commotion grew louder.

"Let's find out," Finn said, already moving towards the source of the disturbance. Together, they pushed through the door, leaving the chill of the morgue behind, before heading along a short corridor at the front of the diminutive hospital and then stepping into uncertainty and the chaos that awaited them outside.

"Why do I get the feeling that..."

Finn's sentence was cut abruptly short by the sound of raised voices and a commotion outside.

"Help!" a voice shouted.

Both Finn and Amelia snapped to attention, their training kicking in. Without a word, they moved in tandem towards the door—the urgency of the situation propelling them forward.

"Stay behind me," Finn murmured, reaching instinctively for the sidearm he no longer carried.

"You stay behind me," Amelia retorted.

They burst through the doors, the brightness of the hallway momentarily disorienting after the gloom of the morgue. Shouts echoed down the corridor, the sound growing louder as they approached the hospital's main entrance.

"Over there!" Amelia pointed ahead where a group of people had gathered, some of them shouting.

"Keep your eyes open," Finn advised, scanning the area for any immediate threat. His heart raced. "This could be one of Vilne's tricks."

CHAPTER EIGHT

From the shadowed eaves of a nearby building, he watched them emerge—Finn Wright, with his FBI-honed alertness, and Inspector Amelia Winters, whose keen gaze seemed almost to brush against him in its sweep over the crowd. The killer's fingers twitched involuntarily as they steadied the binoculars, the tool of anonymity that kept him invisible among the living.

The killer listened as well as looked, and could here the voices shouting, carried by the cold winter air.

"Keep back, please," Finn's voice was authoritative, slicing through the thickening tension like a scalpel. His stance was wide, arms raised as he faced the agitated assembly that had gathered outside the morgue.

"Everyone will get answers, but we need space to work," Amelia added, her tone firm yet edged with a thread of empathy.

"Answers," the killer muttered to himself, the word tasting sour on his tongue. "They want answers that could unravel everything." He felt the unease clawing at him, the disquiet that had taken roost in his chest since he had left the castle grounds. Within him, justification waged a silent war with the remnants of conscience, both vying for dominance.

The killer moved from behind a car and then to another to get closer. Just close enough to hear every word.

"Sir, I understand you're upset, but escalating this won't help," Finn continued, addressing a burly man whose face was flushed red with anger.

"Upset?" the man bellowed. "Do you realize what this idiot has done?"

The killer's attentions moved to another man. A man he knew well. An infamous real estate agent who had represented the Richmonds. Now, the man was clearly under threat from a small group of men outside of the hospital.

"Please, let us do our job. We are on your side," Amelia interjected before the man could go on, her hand reaching out in a calming gesture. There was a practiced grace to her movements that belied the urgency of the situation.

"Side..." the killer echoed softly, an ironic smile playing on his lips as he shifted his weight from one foot to the other. In his mind's eye, he saw the layout of the castle, the careful steps he had taken, every precaution meticulously planned. Yet here were these two, capable and determined, perhaps even enough to be problematic. And all because Thomas Richmond had spotted him through a window in the library. That had meant improvising. The original intention was to make the murder look like an accident, but that was impossible after that. Still, Thomas had to go one way or another because he was defacing a castle of historical importance. The legendary resting place of King Arthur himself, and all the history that had passed after that.

How dare he do such a thing.

The killer's attention switched once again to the altercation.

"You're not as clever as the papers make out," the man shot back at Amelia, jabbing a finger towards her from distance.

"Look," Finn cut in, his voice carried by a light wind, stepping closer to the man, his eyes locked onto his in a way that commanded attention. "We know why you are angry. We get it. But two people are already dead, I think the area has seen enough violence, don't you? And it's hardly justice."

"Justice," the killer repeated under his breath, the word resonating with him on a perverse level. It reminded him of the justifications he had constructed, the narrative he told himself about setting right a terrible wrong. No. They wouldn't understand. They couldn't.

"Let's talk this through," Amelia urged, her voice a soothing balm amid the cacophony of murmurs and sobs from the crowd.

"Please help me, for God's sake!?" The real estate broker shouted, practically cowering from the burly man.

Finn looked around and glanced momentarily down the street towards where the killer hid. The killer withdrew slightly, retreating further into the shadows. He thought of the blood that had been spilled, of the necessity of his actions. Outsider though he was, his confidence hadn't waned—no, he was too meticulous, too careful to be caught. Yet as he watched Finn and Amelia, a sliver of doubt pierced his resolve, the vague notion that he might have to act again to ensure his secrets remained buried.

With that chilling prospect, he turned and melded into the anonymity of the street, leaving behind the scene that broke into shouts of desperation between the men in front of the hospital—all orchestrated by the very hands now stuffed into his pockets.

CHAPTER NINE

Finn felt like this was the last thing they needed, stopping a fight in the fading light of day, the hospital's sterile tranquility behind them now replaced by the chaotic din of raised voices and unchecked anger. Two robust figures were posturing like territorial animals before a sharply dressed man who looked sheet white with nerves. They had been trying to calm the situation, but it was getting worse.

"Ye bloodsucker! It's 'cause o' you we've got bodies piling up!" one of the burly men bellowed, his face ruddy with indignation.

"Your renovations are diggin' up more than dirt, you heartless swine!" The second man spat the words out as if they left a foul taste in his mouth, his glare fixed on the real estate agent.

"Well, are you going to arrest them? They are threatening me," the man in the suit asked.

"If we have to," Amelia replied.

"Enough of this nonsense!" the man in the suit continued. "I have worked in this area as a real estate agent for ten years. The market dictates progress, not superstitions!" retorted the real estate agent, his accent crisp and out of place amid the rural tones of the locals. His hands gestured wildly, exacerbating the situation rather than calming it.

Finn scanned the growing crowd, noting the way some onlookers clutched each other, whispering fears and suspicions. There was a tangible tension here, a community pushed to the brink, their frustrations now personified in the figure of the real estate agent. Nearby, the shadow of Richmond Castle dominated the darkening skies.

Amelia's eyes flicked between the men, as if assessing their body language, the set of their shoulders, the clenches of their fists. She was ready to intervene to prevent the boiling pot from spilling over. Finn admired her coolness; she was a lighthouse in this storm of human emotion.

"Hey! Let's all take a breath here," Finn called out, his voice authoritative yet not confrontational, stepping forward with a peacekeeper's grace. "Nobody's solving anything with shouting."

"Stand down, gentlemen," Amelia added, projecting confidence as she positioned herself beside Finn, an unspoken signal of solidarity. "We're all looking for answers, not more problems."

The locals turned towards Finn and Amelia, their faces etched with the lines of hard living and harder losses. They seemed momentarily taken aback by the authority in the investigators' presence. But the real estate agent used the brief lull to compose himself, straightening his tie as though preparing for another round of verbal jousting.

"Very well, inspector," he said with a clipped tone, addressing Amelia directly. "But I expect these... individuals to be handled appropriately."

Finn watched the agent carefully, detecting the underlying tension in his stance, the way his eyes flickered with something more than just indignation. This was a man who was used to getting his way, no matter the cost, and right now, he seemed more concerned with his own status than the gravity of the situation at hand. The question lingered in the air: How much did profit weigh against the value of human life?

Finn felt a little disdain for the man, as he only seemed brave once in the company of police officers, he had been almost cowardly before he knew he was safe. Now, he was being demanding and trying to wield authority. Finn had encountered that kind of a man many times before, and it was not a personality type he admired. It was too slimy to him.

"Handled *appropriately*," Amelia echoed, her words a promise rather than a mere assurance. Finn respected that about her—the commitment to justice, no matter where the investigation led.

As the sun dipped lower, casting long shadows across the street, it was clear that this was more than just a simple dispute. It was a clash of values, a community grappling with change, and somewhere in the middle lay the truth about the murders that had brought Finn and Amelia to this point. Finn's most pertinent question that was on his mind, was why were they fighting outside the hospital? Did they know the morgue was there? Did they know the bodies of Lily and Thomas Richmond were only a couple of corridors away?

The air was charged with accusation, the words of the locals sharp as shards of glass against the silence that had befallen the evening. Finn's gaze cut through the crowd, each face a mosaic of bile and anger, as he and Amelia stepped forward, their presence commanding yet non-threatening.

"Everyone, please!" Amelia raised her voice, the note of authority clear, her hands extended in a gesture of peace. "Let's take this down a notch."

The real estate agent, standing firm in the eye of the storm, adjusted his suit jacket with a flick of his wrist. His voice sliced through the unrest, drenched in self-importance. "I am Gregory Harding," he announced, his chin tilting upwards. "I liaise directly with the castle's proprietors. I know it's you people who have blood on your hands—Lily and Thomas were innocent, and I will see justice served!"

Finn scrutinized Harding, noting how his assertion fanned the flames of discontent. The agent's demeanor was more than just professional pride; it was an armor to shield his own interests.

"Gregory, is it?" Finn's tone was calm but edged. "We'll need to discuss your—"

Before Finn could finish, one of the local men lunged forward, his fist arcing towards Harding with the ferocity of a cornered animal. "You won't pin this on us!"

Action erupted. Finn's reflexes, honed from years in the field, snapped like a whip. He caught the assailant's arm mid-swing, twisting it behind his back with swift precision. The man's momentum faltered, and he stumbled, pain etching his features.

"Enough!" Finn's command ricocheted off the stone walls of the morgue. He held the man firmly, controlling his movements.

"Amelia!" he called, without taking his eyes off the subdued attacker.

In fluid motion, Amelia approached, her handcuffs glinting faintly in the waning light. She secured them around the man's wrists with efficiency, her movements unhesitating. "You're under arrest for assault," she stated, her voice devoid of triumph, but laced with resolve.

"Let me go! He's the one tearing our heritage apart!" the man cried out, his voice hoarse with desperation.

Harding straightened his jacket once more, his eyes darting to the restrained figure, then to Amelia. "See to it that he's charged," he insisted, brushing off nonexistent dust from his sleeve as if to rid himself of the altercation's taint.

Finn exchanged a look with Amelia, a silent communication they'd perfected over several case's together. Finn could tell that Amelia was annoyed with the man's tone as much as he was.

"Listen up!" Amelia shouted. "This man is being arrested, anyone else fancy a night in the cells?"

The cacophony from the previously unruly crowd had begun to dissipate, replaced by the sharp clack of boots on pavement as two constables approached with purpose from the hospital.

"Inspector Winters," Amelia said to them, showing her ID. "Are you with the Richmond investigation?"

"No, ma'am," one of the constables said. "But we're aware of your presence. The hospital is on our rounds because of the A & E. We heard what was happening and thought we'd assist."

"Thank you," Amelia said. "Take those two into custody."

Amelia pointed to the man being restrained and the other burly figure who had been shouting with him.

"This one for assault," Amelia said. "And the other for a breach of the peace."

"Wait a minute!" the other man. "I 'aven't done anythin'!"

"Tell you're solicitor that," Finn said. "There's been a double murder at Richmond Castle, and here you are threatening someone else associated with it. Seems to me, you are a suspect we will need to interview in due course."

"No!" was all the man could say.

"Take them to Wellhaven Police Station," Amelia said.

With efficient movements, they escorted the two local men away, whose protests and accusations had become muffled under the stern gaze of authority. The air felt suddenly thick with the scent of tension and rain-soaked asphalt.

"Inspector Winters, I expect charges to be pressed against that brute," the real estate broker, Harding, said, adjusting his tie with fingers that betrayed a hint of unsteadiness.

"Mr. Harding," Amelia replied, her voice steady despite the surge of adrenaline she was working to quell, "how well did you know Thomas and Lily?"

"We were close," he stated firmly, locking eyes with her in an attempt to convey sincerity. "Close enough to understand the weight of their loss. And believe me, I won't rest until whoever has done this is behind bars."

Finn, who had been observing the exchange with a scrutinous gaze, stepped forward. "Then you wouldn't mind answering some questions. Why are you hear at this hospital?"

"The Richmond's don't have any family here," he answered. "I received a call and was asked to identify the bodies, given I am the person closest to them in the UK, both personally and in a business sense."

Finn nodded. "Another thing I'm particularly interested in—"

"Inspector Winters!" The urgency in one of the constable's voice sliced through Finn's words as he re-emerged from the hospital. "There's trouble at the castle, a mob's gathered, and it's getting out of hand. Thought you should know."

"Understood," Amelia responded, her mind already racing through potential scenarios. She gave Harding a curt nod. "We'll discuss your involvement later. For now, we have another situation to address." He handed over a card.

"You'll need to do better than that, you can go with one of the constables to give a statement about this altercation," Amelia explained.

He sighed. "Is that *really* necessary right now?"

"Yes," came Amelia's short reply.

She and Finn moved over to Amelia's parked service car.

"I'll drive this time," Amelia said as they both got in.

"I love it when you get all biblical," Finn quipped, sitting in the passenger seat.

"Inspector Winters," Mr. Harding called out just as Amelia was about to turn the ignition. "May I accompany you instead? There are details—pertinent information—I believe could aid your investigation. And I think you should hear it."

"Couldn't hurt," Finn said in a quiet voice to Amelia. "But your call."

"Get in," she said, jerking her head toward the back seat.

Rushing over, Harding got into the back seat. Once he had settled in, an impatient click of the seat belt signaling his readiness, Amelia started the engine, and the car hummed to life beneath them. Finn observed her. She reversed smoothly, her fingers firm on the wheel, eyes flicking to the rearview mirror where she could see Harding's sharp profile.

Finn knew when she had fire in her belly.

"Mind telling us what this crucial information is?" Finn asked, turning slightly to address the man behind them as they drove.

"Let's just say..." Harding hesitated, the weight of his words hanging between them, "...the ties that bind us to the castle are not just financial but historical. And sometimes, history has a way of resurfacing at the most inconvenient times."

"Sounds like you have a degree in vagueness from Vague University," Finn said, his gaze narrowing slightly as he processed the implications. "Does everyone around here have to talk like they are in Victorian detective novel?"

The roads darkened, and Amelia turned on her headlights, speeding to the castle to find out why trouble had visited there for the second time in 24 hours.

CHAPTER TEN

Finn stared at the coming night outside as Amelia's hands gripped the steering wheel, navigating the serpentine roads that led to the castle. His eyes scanned the horizon. It felt bleaker than usual, a stagnant combination of recent events and knowing Vilne was out there hiding somewhere, ready to strike.

He kept catching glimpses of Amelia as she turned her ear towards the back seat. Their passenger, cloaked in the musky scent of ambition tainted with fear, was the real estate broker—a man whose silhouette seemed to shrink under scrutiny.

"Mr. Harding," Amelia began, her tone sharpening like a blade against a whetstone, "about the murders last night. Where exactly were you?"

The real estate broker, Mr. Harding, recoiled as if struck, his face contorting in shock. "I—murder? I'm a businessman, Inspector Winters, not some thug." His voice climbed an octave, betraying a hint of desperation.

"Interesting defense," Finn interjected turning towards him. "I've seen plenty of cut-throat businessmen in my time. That's not an alibi."

"Fine," Mr. Harding spat out, his composure fraying at the edges. "I was at a dinner party, networking for potential clients until midnight. After which, I went straight home. I don't want the news spread because it was with a rival company, I'm thinking of moving on, but until I know for certain, I don't want my employers to know."

Finn nodded slowly, knowing that it was likely such an alibi was true. However, he and Amelia would need to send some constables to question witnesses and verify it while they contended with other aspects of the case.

Amelia focused on the winding path ahead, but Finn could tell that she was making mental notes of the man's responses, measuring the weight of truth against self-preservation. Whenever she bit her bottom lip in deep thought, Finn knew she was thinking something through.

"Did you see or speak to anyone about Thomas or Lily during this party?" she pressed on. "About the renovations at the castle? That must be pretty big news in the area, and as big a client as it gets."

"Absolutely not," Mr. Harding replied, a little too quickly. "I had no reason to. I was there simply to socialize and network with a potential employer."

"Yet that employer must be impressed that you have the castle in your portfolio?" Amelia's voice was cool, calculated.

"So what if I did mention it? I count the Richmond's as dear friends after working with them for so long, but the problems with the castle and the local reaction... To be honest, I'll be glad to be away from it." The broker's words came out rehearsed, like he'd been expecting this conversation.

"Right," Finn murmured, skepticism lacing his thoughts. 'And now you will be done with it, at least whatever the Richmond's vision was for the castle.' Finn reminded himself, recalling the countless faces of guilt he'd seen before—none of them wore a sign declaring their deeds.

As the castle loomed into view, its half-painted walls like a patchwork, a grotesque Frankenstein against the skyline, Finn couldn't help but sense the castle was at the core of it all.

"You said you had something important to tell us, Harding?" Finn said as Amelia stopped at the Castle Richmond estate gates, showed her badge to a constable, and continued along a winding road through woodland, now more threatening in the near dark.

"Enlighten us, Mr. Harding," Amelia's voice was as sharp as the chill that had settled in the car, "why do you reckon Thomas and Lily were murdered? And what do you know about it?"

Mr. Harding shifted uncomfortably in his seat, his eyes darting to the window before locking with Amelia's in the rearview mirror. "The locals," he began, "And not just any. Activists! They break into estates and threaten anyone who wants to, in their eyes, deface their heritage. They despised what the couple planned for the castle. They see it as vandalism."

"Vandalism is a strong word," Finn interjected as Amelia's hands steadied the wheel turning a blind corner on the narrow road leading up to the castle. "These people, do they hate any changes so much that they would turn violent?"

"Progress is always hindered by the blind," Mr. Harding countered, a trace of defiance in his tone. "Perhaps it's time this area begins to think about the future rather than clinging to the past. My point is, if you find these locals, you will find the murderer among them."

Finn pondered the truth in those words. History had its place, but so did moving forward. Yet, where was the line drawn between preservation and evolution?

The car crested the final hill, revealing the castle's outline, sprawling across the center of the estate. But the majesty of the ancient stone was overshadowed by the agitation unfolding at its gates. A group of locals had gathered within the estate, brandishing placards like medieval shields; their slogans screamed resistance against the renovations.

"Look! There they are!" the broker said with disdain.

"Looks like we've stumbled upon a siege," Finn quipped, trying to ease the tension that buzzed through the car like static.

"Hardly a siege when the walls have already been breached," Amelia replied, eyeing the crowd with an investigator's curiosity.

"This looks like it could get out of hand," said Finn, wondering if Harding's presence might incense the crowd.

"We're not getting through that," Amelia said. "I'll park here."

Amelia pulled up near the people, who were still shouting and holding placards.

Finn's gaze lingered on the faces in the crowd—contorted by passion, fear, and anger. Each person there bore the weight of their convictions, and each conviction was a potential lead to a very real killer.

"Let's hope these protesters stick to wielding signs and not something sharper," he muttered, more to himself than anyone else.

"Hope so," Amelia agreed, her hand already on the door handle, ready to step into the heart of the conflict.

Finn stepped out of the car, his boots sinking slightly into the soft earth. The sky loomed overhead, a tapestry of gray threatening rain, as if nature itself shared in the crowd's tumultuous mood. He approached the perimeter where the protesters stood like an ancient army protecting their besieged fortress.

"Good morning," he called out, attempting diplomacy over the din of discontented voices. "I'm Finn Wright with the Home Office. I'm here to help sort this mess—"

"Help?" A voice cut through, sharp as a blade. An elderly woman, her hair a wild halo of white, jabbed a finger in his direction. "You lot are all the same! American money tearing at the fabric of our heritage!"

"Ma'am, I assure you—" Finn's words faltered as more voices joined the chorus of accusation. He hadn't reckoned that his accent would provoke such a reaction.

"Another Yank come to trample on history!" shouted a man with a face as red as the bricks of the castle behind him.

Finn's jaw tightened. He wasn't one for losing his cool, but ignorance bit at him harder than the chill in the air. His past was littered with debris from misconceptions; he didn't need more piled on here.

"Listen," he tried again, "I understand your concerns, really, I do—"

"Concerns?" The woman spat the word as if it were poison. "Our history isn't some concern—it's our soul!"

"But both of the Richmonds are dead," Finn said. "Why protest like this?"

"Because no doubt the castle will still go to another outsider!" a shout rose. "And they need to know they won't get away with vandalizing King Arthur's resting place!"

"It should be in Cornish hands!" another yell went up, followed by some cheers.

Finn knew there was going to be no reasoning with them.

"We need through," Amelia said loudly, seemingly losing patience. "Police business."

"Hey!" another voice yelled from the crowd. "That's Harding in the back of that car!"

Harding, clearly not thinking, or overestimating how much protection he had, stepped out of the car.

"Scum!" someone shouted.

"Traitor!" another in a barrage of insults.

"None of you have even got it right!" the broker bellowed above the hostility. "The castle was going to bring in tourists with its unique look. It was an art project!"

"Art? More like desecration!" The retort came fast and fierce, followed by a surge of collective fury that rippled through the crowd like a wave poised to crash.

"This is going to get out of hand," Amelia said quietly to Finn. "We need to either find a way through or get Harding somewhere else."

"I don't know," Finn replied. "Kind of would be enjoyable to see what the locals do with Harding."

"No time for jokes, Finn!" Amelia said, harshly. "If something happens to him under our watch, we'll be off the case for sure."

"Our past! Our past!" a chant went up. Some of the crowd moved forward towards the car where Harding stood.

Suddenly, he didn't look so confident in his safety anymore.

Finn squared his shoulders, ready to intervene, when suddenly an egg arced through the air. It connected with the broker's suit with a satisfying splat, yolk dripping down the fine fabric like liquid gold.

"Damn it!" the broker exclaimed, wiping at the mess, face contorted not in humiliation but in anger.

Four constables now appeared from the door of the castle.

"Make way! Make way! They shouted, parting the crowd.

The crowd seemed satisfied by laughing at Harding's fine suit.

"Let's get inside before they change their minds!" Finn ordered, the situation spiraling beyond verbal spats, every second increasing the risk of someone getting hurt.

He moved, positioning himself between the broker and the crowd, his instincts kicking in. He was no stranger to volatile situations—the memories of which crawled beneath his skin, urging caution—and this was escalating into dangerous territory.

"Come on, let's get you cleaned up," Amelia said, a note of urgency in her voice as she grasped the broker's arm, guiding him away from the fray.

"Watch it!" a protester warned, and Finn cast a backward glance, noting the set jaws and clenched fists.

"A nice hose would sort you all out," he muttered, his mind already cataloging faces, storing away the raw emotion etched into them. This was more than just a simple disturbance. It was a town's outcry, a festering wound of resentment. And somewhere in the turmoil lay clues to a darker truth—a motive steeped in the kind of passion that could drive a person to murder.

An oaken door, ancient and brooding, loomed ahead as Finn's fingers dug into the broker's slick jacket, propelling him up the stone steps. Amelia was at the other's side, her grip firm, ushering him away from the growing tempest outside.

"Quite the welcome committee," Finn quipped dryly, despite the intensity boiling in his veins. They crossed the threshold, the heavy door closing with a thud that muted the ire of the crowd.

"Should've had them all arrested," the real estate agent spat, shaking off their hands as if the touch were offensive. He straightened his jacket, attempting to salvage what dignity he could. "This is what I get for trying to bring progress to this place."

"Progress doesn't usually come served with an egg," Finn retorted, scanning the grand entrance hall for signs of further trouble. High ceilings echoed back their footsteps, while tapestries seemed to watch in silent judgment. "I kind of respect how good the aim was."

"Never mind the damned egg! You're police, aren't you? Why don't you act like it?" The real estate broker's voice was thick with disdain.

"Because, unlike eggs, we can't just throw people in jail on a whim," Amelia shot back with a calm that belied the tension in her posture. She glanced at Finn, the shared look between them one of weary understanding.

"I'm not technically police," Finn said with a grin. "I'm a consultant detective."

"Whatever," the broker scoffed, flicking a piece of shell from his shoulder. "Just do your job and find out who's behind this madness. And make sure they pay."

"Believe me," Finn said, his eyes narrowing as he surveyed the broker—a man seemingly more concerned with retribution than safety—"nothing gets past us." His mind was already sifting through the incident, plucking at details that seemed incongruent, out of place.

"Good," the broker huffed, but his arrogance couldn't mask a flicker of anxiety. "Because none of this... none of this should be happening to me. And it certainly shouldn't have happened to the Richmonds."

Finn's gaze lingered on the broker, noting the shift. Fear often wore many masks, and beneath the arrogance, there might just be something worth uncovering.

Amelia leaned against the cold stone wall, arms folded as she fixed the real estate broker with a steely gaze. "We need to know who would take things to the extreme. Who hated the renovations enough to commit murder?"

The broker's lips curled in a sneer. "I warned them," he said, his voice dripping with self-importance. "I told Thomas that not everyone was thrilled about their grand designs. But they were too wrapped up in their visions of grandeur. I told him there was a middle way, a way to update the castle without angering people. One piece at a time, so they could get used to it. But he didn't listen."

Finn stepped closer, the click of his shoes on the marble floor resonating through the cavernous space. He observed the broker's face, watching for any crack in the facade. "People knew you immediately," he asked. "That means there's history. Did you receive threats?"

"Threats came from every corner—the protectors of history, conservationists, even people who just don't like change." The broker's eyes flitted away for a moment before locking back onto Finn's, a challenge laid bare.

"Exactly how severe were these threats?" Amelia pressed, moving forward until she was mere inches from the broker.

With an exaggerated shrug, the broker pulled out his smartphone, swiped with a thumb coated in arrogance, and presented the screen to them. A wry laugh escaped him as he did so. "Take a look at this," he said.

Amelia took the phone, and Finn peered over her shoulder. The inbox was a cesspool of vitriol—messages stacked upon messages, each laden with more malice than the last. It was a tapestry of threats woven with hatred, a digital monument to the darkest sides of humanity.

"Christ," muttered Finn under his breath. Every line was a potential lead, every curse a possible clue. "We're going to need to go through all of these."

"Be my guest." The broker's tone was flippant, but Finn detected a sliver of satisfaction—as if he enjoyed the idea of them wading through the mire on his behalf.

"Alright," Amelia said, her voice steady as she handed the phone back. "We'll need full access to your emails. All of it."

"Fine," the broker snapped, snatching the phone back. He pulled out a business card and a small pen from his inside pocket and scribbled down something, handing it back to Amelia. "That's my login details. Just find whoever's responsible. I've got other properties to deal with, and I'd quite like to do that without ending up dead!"

"He's right," Finn said, turning to Amelia. "We need to go through these messages, certainly before anyone throes more eggs at Harding here."

"Or bacon," Amelia said. "Soon it'll be a full English breakfast."

"This is hardly a time to joke," the real estate agent said.

"Our constables will take you out of here, Mr Harding," Amelia said. "Once the crowd dies down. It's nearly night, so I wouldn't think they'll be out there much longer."

"Can I drive this time? It clears my head?" Finn asked.

"Sure," Amelia said.

"I mean, if you'd rather rock, papers, scissor it for the privilege?" Finn grinned.

"You can drive," Amelia laughed.

Then, they were off. Finn and Amelia stepped back towards the door and looked out. The constables were still struggling with the crowd, but there was a way through. Quickly, they rushed through it, ignoring the taunts from the crowd, rushing towards their car to see what hidden clues could be found in the Harding's emails.

CHAPTER ELEVEN

The cold, icy rain lashed against the windshield with a relentless rhythm, blurring the quaint streetlamps of the village as they sped past. Finn's hands gripped the steering wheel, his knuckles white from the effort to keep the car steady on the slick cobblestones. Beside him, Amelia's profile was illuminated intermittently by the passing lights, her gaze fixed on the road ahead.

"Feels wrong, doesn't it?" Amelia broke the silence, her voice cutting through the drumming of the downpour. "Leaving the real estate bloke back there with that mob."

Finn chuckled dryly, a brief smirk playing on his lips as he navigated a tight bend. "If he's not safe in a castle, then where is he safe?" he said, the irony not lost on him. His eyes lingered for a moment on the rear-view mirror, where the faint outline of the ancient fortress loomed like a brooding sentinel in the distance.

"True," Amelia conceded, tucking a stray lock of red hair behind her ear. "But still, those protesters were quite heated."

"A few of your finest are with him," Finn remarked, easing off the accelerator as they approached a pedestrian crossing. "And honestly, trying to escort him out in front of them might've just thrown fuel on the fire. Best to let things cool down a bit."

Amelia nodded, folding her arms as she settled back into her seat. The glow from the dashboard cast shifting shadows across her face, highlighting her furrowed brow and the determined set of her jaw. She was tough, Finn had to give her that; not many could handle the kind of pressure this case was exerting.

"Do you think the murderer might be among these emails?" Finn asked.

"Are you coming around to the idea then that Vilne isn't the killer?" Amelia answered with a question.

"I don't know," Finn sighed. "I still think he's involved."

Amelia said nothing, but Finn knew how she felt.

They drove on in silence for a while, each lost in thought as the wipers swept back and forth in a futile attempt to clear their the way. Sometimes Finn felt his mind was just as obscured, but he abstained from making a "wipers for my brain" joke.

The wipers battled against the persistent drizzle, leaving streaks across the windshield that distorted the glow of streetlights. Finn could feel the weariness in his bones as he drove, the kind that came not just from long hours, but from the weight of unsolved questions pressing on his mind.

"Keeps coming back to me," Finn murmured, more to himself than to Amelia, "the choice of weapon. Medieval, isn't it? A bit dramatic for a modern-day killing."

"Symbolic?" Amelia suggested, her gaze steady on the road ahead.

"Has to be. Whoever did this wanted to make a point." Finn's fingers tightened on the steering wheel. "Thomas and Lily were altering the castle's identity. It's like...like they were cut down for not respecting its history."

"Preservation by bloodshed," Amelia remarked dryly.

"Exactly." Finn exhaled slowly. "It's someone who sees themselves as the guardian of that place. Our killer doesn't deal in renovations—they deal in retribution."

Amelia glanced at him, her eyes reflecting the passing lights. "Speaking of guardians, what about you and Demi? When we catch Max Vilne, are you planning to leave the country with her?"

Finn's grip on the wheel faltered for a fraction of a second before he caught himself. He peered out into the dark, where the silhouettes of buildings slipped past them like silent sentinels. "I don't know, Amelia. I really don't."

"Is it about her safety?" she pressed gently, sensing there was more beneath the surface.

"Partly." Finn's voice was thick with unspoken thoughts. He darted a glance at Amelia, noting the concern etched on her features. "It's about making sure everyone I care about is safe. But how do you safeguard people from a man like Vilne? He's not just a killer; he's a force of nature—unpredictable, unstoppable."

"Then we'll have to be the immovable object," Amelia replied with quiet conviction.

"Quite the pair we'd make," Finn said with a half-smile, though his eyes remained shadowed by doubt.

"Unstoppable force meets immovable object. Sounds like a bad thriller novel," Amelia said, trying to lighten the mood.

"Or the plot of our lives lately." Finn's smile faded as quickly as it had appeared. "Let's just focus on one step at a time."

"Agreed." Amelia nodded, then turned her attention back to the road, leaving Finn to the storm brewing within.

The heavy silence hung between them like the dense fog that clung to the rolling hills outside. The car's interior light cast a soft glow on Amelia's face as she scrolled through her phone, her fingers making short, efficient swipes across the screen. Finn found himself studying the way her eyebrows furrowed in concentration, a testament to her unyielding determination.

"Got something?" Finn broke the silence without turning his gaze from the winding road ahead.

"Actually, yes." Amelia's voice sliced through the stillness with an edge of triumph. "I've just gained access to the real estate broker's emails."

"Good," Finn replied, the corners of his mouth curling into a half-smile at her evident satisfaction. He shifted gears, the engine growling in response as they navigated another sharp bend. "We'll comb through them once we're back."

"Could be the break we need," Amelia said, locking her phone and placing it in her lap. Her eyes, now free from their digital burden, met Finn's for a fleeting moment before he returned his focus to the road.

"Before that," Finn said, his mind churning through the possibilities, "we should talk to the bloke who took a swing at our dear broker outside the morgue. If he's willing to get physical in broad daylight, there's no telling what else he's capable of."

"People are willing to be violent for the strangest of things," Amelia murmured, contemplation clear in her tone. "Sometimes I wonder if we're any different."

"We are," Finn nodded. "Rage can make a person cross lines they never thought they'd dare to, but we would never intentionally hurt someone that didn't have it coming. And if this guy is connected to Vilne..."

"Then we might be looking at more than just a passionate outburst," Amelia finished the thought, her analytical mind already piecing together the implications.

"Right." Finn glanced at her. Their eyes met and they smiled. It was like electricity. But it was as if Amelia felt it, too. She moved her glance to the window to her side.

Finn's grip on the steering wheel tightened, the leather creaking under his fingers. The silence returned, unfilled by words, stretching out like the winding country roads before them. He swallowed the discomfort, restless energy buzzing beneath his skin, a relentless current urging him toward action.

"I wonder if this thing works," he muttered, more to himself than to Amelia, and reached for the radio. With a click, the car filled with the soft hum of classical music, notes from a piano concerto unfolding in delicate waves.

The vehicle surged forward as Finn pressed harder on the accelerator, the engine growling in harmony with the tense forces inside of him.

"Speeding won't solve the case, Wright," Amelia said, though her tone lacked any real admonishment. "It won't solve... Anything."

Finn knew what she was talking about. The connection between them is as deep as any valley.

"Maybe not," he admitted, "but it'll get us out of here faster." His eyes flicked to the rearview mirror, half-expecting to catch sight of trouble tailing them, but the road behind remained empty—a stretch of tarmac bordered by hedgerows and the occasional flash of a field mouse darting for cover.

As they neared the local police station, the last vestiges of twilight clung to the horizon, painting it with hues of fiery orange and dusky pink, though night was overhead already. The day was slipping away, but Finn felt the thrum of anticipation coursing through him. Tonight, they would edge closer to the truth, no matter how perilous the path.

CHAPTER TWELVE

As Finn strode alongside Inspector Amelia through the immaculate corridors of Wellhaven Police Station, he couldn't help but feel the sterility of the place prickle at his senses. The walls gleamed with a clinical whiteness that was almost blinding, and the air carried a faint scent of antiseptic. "This place feels more like a hospital than a police station," he remarked, his voice echoing slightly off the polished floor.

"Was just the same when I started out here," Amelia responded, her heels clicking in rhythm with Finn's footsteps. "The Chief Inspector wouldn't have it any other way. A speck of dust would probably send him into a fit."

"I like a good bit of mess," Finn mused, though his thoughts were elsewhere.

"You're all mess, Finn," Amelia said.

"I don't know how to take that," Finn laughed, feigning offense.

"I mean it in the best possible way."

They approached an interview room where Inspector Wilson stood guard, his posture rigid, eyes sharp as flint and his mustache as gray as they night. "Amelia, Finn," he greeted them, nodding curtly. "I hope you don't mind, I was finishing for the night but found out you had a suspect. He's inside," he added, thumbing towards the closed door.

"Always welcome, Inspector," Finn offered.

"I hear you arrested him outside the morgue?" Wilson asked. "Nothing like the prey coming to you."

"Wilson," Amelia acknowledged with a soft but professional smile. "What do we know about our friend in there?"

"Name's Boris Tanner," Wilson said, handing over a file. Its cover was marked with red flags, indicating a record that was anything but pristine. "His sheet's as dirty as your lot keep this place clean," Finn quipped, leafing through the pages, noting the recurring offenses scrawled across the records.

"Professional protester, or so it seems," Amelia observed, scanning the file over Finn's shoulder. "Trespassing, obstruction, public nuisance..."

"Seems he doesn't take kindly to people buying up historical sites,"

Finn added, his mind already piecing together a profile. "Especially not Richmond Castle."

"Indeed," Wilson confirmed. "And his antics got physical outside the hospital morgue with the Richmond's real estate broker. Not the smartest move."

"Or perhaps the most telling," Finn suggested, his gaze never leaving the file.

"Let's see what Mr. Tanner has to say for himself then," Amelia decided, her tone all business. She was ready to confront whatever lay behind that door, her resolve as unbreakable as the polished surface of the station's floors.

Finn placed the file under his arm, feeling the familiar thrill of the chase ignite within him. As they stepped closer to the interview room, Finn felt the usual surge of adrenaline that accompanied every suspect interview. He had to control that to make sure it didn't cloud his mind.

"Let's hope Mr. Tanner is in a talkative mood," Amelia said, her hand reaching for the door handle.

"Either way," Finn replied, with a glint of determination in his eye, "I have a feeling he knows something."

The door to the interview room swung open with a whisper, a silent testament to the meticulous upkeep of Wellhaven Police Station. Finn Wright stepped through the threshold, his senses immediately sharpening at the sight before him. Boris Tanner sat on the far side of the table, his silhouette rigid and imposing against the stark white of the room.

"Mr. Tanner," Finn greeted, voice steady but not without a hint of steel.

Tanner's response was merely a grunt as he unfolded his arms, resting them on the table with a sense of defiance that bordered on provocation. His eyes, dark pits of intensity, locked onto Finn's, unblinking. The air between them became charged, an invisible current crackling with the tension of unspoken challenges.

Amelia Winters followed suit, the clack of her heels on linoleum tiles punctuating the silence that had settled like dust. She maneuvered around the table with a grace that belied the gravity of the situation, pulling out a chair opposite Tanner. The scrape of metal legs against the floor sounded abnormally loud in the sterile environment.

"Good evening," Amelia said, her voice devoid of any tremor that might betray the high stakes of the interrogation. With a practiced motion, she pressed the button on the recording device situated at the center of the table. A soft beep acknowledged the start of the record.

"Today is the 16th of November, 6:05pm," Amelia announced, enunciating clearly for the sake of the audio log. "I am Inspector Amelia Winters, and with me is consulting detective Finn Wright."

"Present," Finn added, jokingly, raising his arm like a school child only for the file to fall out from under it onto the floor. He quickly picked it up and tried his best to act cool.

As Amelia continued the formalities, Finn took the opportunity to study Tanner more closely. There was something about the way the man sat, an innate resilience reminiscent of ancient walls weathering relentless storms. But beneath the surface, Finn detected the subtlest flicker of uncertainty—a flame that could be fanned into a blaze with the right breath.

Finn's analytical mind began to whir, piecing together Tanner's posture, the set of his jaw, the slightest shift of his weight. Every detail was a clue, every movement a potential piece of the puzzle they were trying to solve. Finn's past may have been marred by personal upheaval and professional setbacks, yet his ability to read people remained undiminished by those stresses. It was this very skill that had once made him a formidable agent, and now, it served as the key to unlocking Tanner's facade.

"Are you comfortable, Mr. Tanner?" Finn asked, his tone deliberately casual.

"Comfort's got nothing to do with it," Tanner retorted, his voice a low rumble. "Let's get on with it."

"Indeed," Amelia concurred, her own scrutiny of Tanner covert yet thorough.

"Very well," Finn agreed, shifting in his seat, ready to dance the delicate tango of interrogation. Tanner might resemble a bull, but Finn and Amelia were matadors, adept in the art of control. They would weave their questions like capes—red flashes of inquiry designed to direct and ultimately, uncover the truth hidden behind Tanner's bullish stance.

Finn's gaze locked onto Boris Tanner. The sterile hum of the police station seemed to recede behind the veil of concentration that descended upon the room. "Mr. Tanner," Finn began, a razor-sharp edge of inquisition to his voice, "I couldn't help but notice you're here without representation."

"Lawyers?" Boris scoffed, a derisive snort escaping him as though the very word tasted sour. "They're just another cog in the bloody machine. I stand for myself." His chin jutted out defiantly, a physical manifestation of his obstinance.

Amelia leaned forward, her elbows resting on the cold metal table, her fingers interlacing with precision. "Let's talk about your altercation with Gregory Harding." Her voice was calm, measured, like the first few drops of rain heralding a storm.

"Private matter," Boris muttered, almost to himself, his arms tightening across his chest as if guarding secrets.

"Private until it spills into public view," Finn countered, leaning back and observing Boris with eyes that missed nothing. "Harding is a real estate broker, isn't he? Represented Thomas and Lily Richmond... recently acquired Richmond Castle before their untimely demise last night."

The words hung heavy in the air, each syllable laden with implication. Finn watched as the muscles in Boris's neck tensed, cords standing out against his skin like rigid sentinels. The man shifted, a subtle redistribution of weight, his feet planted firmly on the ground as if bracing against an unseen force.

"Richmond Castle?" Boris's voice was a low growl, barely contained. "You mean Hemworth Castle." There was a history there, unspoken but palpable. Finn could sense it, smell it—it was the scent of old battles and grievances long-held.

"Richmond Castle, Hemworth Castle," Amelia interjected smoothly, redirecting the conversation with the finesse of a chess master moving a pawn. "Names don't matter as much as the death of two human beings. What we need to know is why you clashed with Harding."

Their suspect's eyes flickered to Amelia, an ember of anger glowing in their depths. "Harding is a vulture, picking over carcasses for profit. But murder?" His voice broke, something raw and unfiltered seeping through. "That's not my type of fight."

"Yet here you are after threatening him outside the hospital," Finn pointed out, the observation sharp as a knife blade. "Your hands aren't clean, Mr. Tanner."

"Clean hands in a dirty world?" Boris sneered, his bravado a brittle shell. "That's a fairy tale, Detective Wright. You should know better."

Amelia's hand hovered above the recording device, a silent sentinel capturing every spoken truth and lie. Finn studied Boris, noting the way his eyes darted, the clench of his jaw. He was searching for cracks in the man's armor, and all it would take was patience—the sort that had been honed in darker times and lonelier places.

"The Richmonds' murder is no fairy tale, Mr. Tanner," Finn said quietly. "And neither will the hefty prison sentence be that follows it."

The interview room was a sterile box, the light too bright and the air tinged with the smell of industrial cleaner. Finn's gaze never left Boris Tanner, whose presence seemed to suck the warmth out of the space. Amelia sat across from Boris, her posture relaxed but her eyes sharp.

"Prison?" Boris's voice boomed suddenly, his fist crashing down on the table with enough force to make the water in the plastic cups ripple. "Been there, done that, got the t-shirt. I'm not going back, and that's why I *wouldn't* kill. But I will say this: It's Hemworth Castle, and it belongs to the community, not to some rich interlopers playing lord and lady!"

Amelia leaned forward, her tone even, yet probing, "Why does that incite such anger in you, Mr. Tanner?"

Boris's chest heaved, his breath coming out in short puffs as if the question had flicked something primal within him. "Angry? You don't know the half of it," he spat out, his eyes blazing with a fire that might have scorched the documents spread out before them. "They stripped the soul from those walls, turned history into a circus for their amusement."

"Would that anger push you towards violence? Towards... hurting the Richmonds?" Amelia's question hung in the air, pointed and heavy.

The realization struck Boris like a physical blow, the color draining from his face as he pieced together the true nature of their interest in him. "You think I killed them?" His voice was a mix of disbelief and indignation, a wildness creeping into his eyes. "I detest what they've done to Richmond, but again, murder? No." He shook his head, a mane of unkempt hair swaying with the motion. "That's not me, and I they wouldn't be worth the time. I didn't do it, but they had it coming."

Finn watched the man carefully, weighing every gesture, every inflection. Boris was a tempest contained within human form, brimming with conviction and fury, but there was a line he claimed not to cross. Was it the truth or just another layer of self-deception?

"That's a lot of hate, my friend. And hate can lead to desperate acts, Mr. Tanner," Finn said calmly. "And desperation can turn even the staunchest moralist into something else entirely. And you don't seem to be the most moral."

"Desperate?" Boris's laugh was devoid of humor. "You think I don't know desperation? But I fight with words and presence, not knives in the dark."

"Words and presence," Finn echoed, letting the silence stretch between them, taut as a wire. He could almost hear the cogs turning in Boris's mind, the struggle to maintain an image of composed defiance.

"Sometimes," Amelia added softly, her eyes locked onto Boris's, "words are not enough for some people. Sometimes actions speak louder, and sometimes they scream."

Boris's hands clenched and unclenched in front of him on the table, the only sign of the turmoil that must be churning inside him. For a moment, Finn wondered just how close to the edge Boris Tanner truly was—and what it would take for him to leap over it.

The chill of the sterile interview room settled around them like a thin frost, seeping into the fibers of Finn's soul. He fixed his gaze on Boris Tanner, who sat rigid across the table, his knuckles pale from the grip he had on his own arms.

"Let's talk about how you happened to be outside that hospital, Boris," Finn began, his tone even but probing. "Quite the coincidence bumping into Gregory Harding there, wouldn't you say?"

The man across from him snorted, a defiant tilt to his head. "Coincidence? Perhaps it's fate. You ever think of that, Mr. Wright?"

"Can't say I've given much credence to fate lately," Finn replied, watching the man's eyes for that flicker of betrayal.

Amelia leaned forward slightly, her voice interjecting smoothly. "It seems more likely that you were following Mr. Harding, given your... interests in the castle's ownership."

"Following?" Boris scoffed, but there was an edge to his voice that danced with the possibility of truth. "I don't need to skulk around like some cheap detective. This is a small place, people cross paths all the time. The hospital is in the town center."

Finn felt the lie before Boris had finished speaking. It fluttered in the air, an unsteady note in the fabric of reality. He let a small pause hang in the room, the hum of the fluorescent lights above providing a subtle soundtrack to their theatrical dance.

"Eleven charges for trespassing, Boris," Finn said as he glanced down at the file sprawled open before him. The dossier on Boris Tanner was a map of confrontations and convictions—lines and contours that shaped the man's history. "And protests, too. It paints a picture, doesn't it? Harding mentioned in passing the idea that some of his critics were activists. Are you part of a group advocating for these historical sites?"

"Advocating?" Boris's brow creased, his lips twisting as if tasting something bitter. "I speak for those without voices, for the stones that have stood longer than any of us. They meant something to our ancestors, and so we should honor them."

"You speak of using your voice, yet here you are," Amelia pointed out, "remaining silent when asked a direct question."

Boris's jaw clenched, the muscle ticking like a clockwork warning of an impending storm. His silence was as loud as any proclamation, echoing off the walls.

"Silence is an answer of its own, Mr. Tanner," Finn added, his eyes never leaving Boris's face. "But not the one we're looking for."

The tension in the room tightened, a bowstring pulled back to its limit.

Finn folded the file and laid it deliberately on the table, its contents a silent testament to the man across from them. Boris Tanner's eyes darted between Finn and Amelia, the air bristling with unspoken tension.

"Mr. Tanner," Finn began, his voice steady as if anchoring himself in the room's growing unease, "you're currently our prime suspect in the murders of Lily and Thomas Richmond."

Boris recoiled as if physically struck, his chair scraping against the pristine floor of the police station. "I didn't do it!" he blurted, his voice a mix of fear and defiance. "There's no evidence."

Amelia leaned forward, her gaze unwavering. "You have a motive, Boris. The sale of that castle... it's a symbol to you, isn't it?"

"Symbols don't kill people," Boris spat out.

"Maybe not," Finn interjected smoothly, thinking back to what the caretaker of Richmond castle had told him. "But someone was seen photographing the estate before the murders—trespassing. Oddly enough, that person matches your description."

Finn was bending the truth.

"That's rubbish," Boris protested, but there was a tremor in his voice, a crack in his facade.

"Is it?" Finn's question hung in the room like smoke. He could sense Boris's resolve beginning to fracture; the man's certainty had given way to doubt, and in that doubt, Finn saw his opportunity.

"I... I have an alibi," Boris said. "My ex-wife can vouch that I stayed with her the last few days and never left her house once."

Finn grinned. "Nice to see you reconciling with your ex, but I'm not sure how believable the word of your ex-wife will be in the face of any evidence we find." Finn thought for a moment. If the alibi *was* real, then perhaps Boris wasn't the murderer, but could lead them to him. They'd need to send someone from Wellhaven to interview the ex.

"You won't see any CCTV of me making my way to the castle or anything," Boris said, a little more confidently this time.

"Let's say I believe you," Finn said, leaning back in his chair. "You are heavily connected to the activist movement in the area, aren't you?"

"So?"

"If you're not guilty," Amelia interjected, "then it stands to reason you might know who is. You know, covering up a murder is almost as bad as committing one."

Boris went red in the face. "I haven't covered up for anyone!"

"Give us your phone, Boris," Finn coaxed, a hint of reassurance lacing his tone. "Let us see who else shares your passion for these causes."

"Like hell I will," Boris growled, yet his hands betrayed him, moving hesitantly toward his pocket.

"Think about it," Finn pressed, his own hand open, inviting trust where there was none. "If you're innocent, what harm is there? If you're not, we'll take it as evidence anyway and get a court order to search its contents. Is protecting someone else who might be a murderer worth going down for it?"

The silence stretched, filled only by the distant hum of the station around them. Finally, Boris's phone landed with a soft thud in Finn's waiting palm. His fingers danced over the screen, forwarding the list of contacts to his email—a digital breadcrumb trail leading to unknown places.

"I don't know who the killer is," he said. "And I don't feel bad for the Richmonds after what they did. But I won't go down for something I had nothing to do with."

"Thank you, Boris. That will be all for now," Finn said, handing back the empty shell of the phone.

As they stepped outside, Finn caught Amelia's eye. "Can we book him for assault," he said quietly. "Hold him for twenty-four hours? Just until we eliminate him as a suspect."

"We can, but there are limits," Amelia replied. "At least now we have two important things to search, Hardings' emails, and Tanner's phone messages. Maybe they'll line up and we'll find the same person in both."

They moved through the station with purpose, a shared

determination fueling their steps.

Each name on Boris's contact list was a thread in a larger tapestry—one that, when unraveled, might reveal the truth behind the castle walls. For now, though, those threads lay dormant in his inbox, waiting to be pulled.

CHAPTER THIRTEEN

Finn sat frustratingly before an aging desktop, its fan emitting a persistent hum as he sifted through digital records. He still couldn't shake the weakness he felt inside of himself from his encounter with Vilne. The drug and his relentless pursuit of Vilne had both left him on the point of exhaustion.

But he had to keep going.

Across from him, Amelia leaned over her own workstation, her fingers a blur across the keyboard. The computer room at Wellhaven Police Station was a stark box of fluorescents and filing cabinets, the air tinged with the scent of overheated electronics and stale coffee.

"Maybe we should use the computers at the constabulary in Garden City," Finn sighed. "At least they'd have been made in this century."

"They're not that old," Amelia replied. "I know HQ is just another thirty minutes from here, but I think it's good to stay as local to the case as possible."

Finn leaned back in his chair, putting his hands behind his head. "If this takes any longer, I'm going to have to put this computer out of its misery."

Time continued on again, but their conversation fell off like a cliff.

"It's got to be someone else," Amelia said, breaking the silence that had fallen between them like a heavy curtain. "If one of these blokes is our killer, then it's not Vilne standing over our shoulders."

Finn glanced up, his eyes narrowing as he digested her words. "Vilne doesn't need to bloody his own hands—not until it pleases him," he replied, his voice low and even. "He's a puppeteer, Amelia. He could have anyone on this list dancing on his strings, waiting for the moment to strike."

She leaned back in her chair, considering. "You think one of these men...?"

"Potentially," Finn muttered, scrolling through rows of names that blurred into one another, each a potential link in a chain leading back to Max Vilne. He clicked on a name, bringing up a file filled with dates and offenses. The cursor blinked a steady pulse in the dim room.

"Remember, Vilne likes control," Finn continued, tapping a key emphatically as if punctuating his point. "He's out there, moving unseen, manipulating events like a grand master."

"Maybe," Amelia conceded, her gaze locked on her screen as she cross-referenced another name against police databases. "But we have to consider every possibility. You can't just—"

"Can't just what?" Finn interjected, leaning forward so that the light caught the hard lines of his face. "Underestimate him? I don't plan to. Not anymore."

Amelia met his stare with equal intensity, her eyes reflecting the screen's glow. "Neither do I. But we need evidence, Finn. Concrete proof, not just theories."

The computer room was a sterile bubble, punctuated by the soft hum of machines and the occasional click of a mouse. Finn's gaze was locked to the screen where digits and names morphed into potential leads, each one a thread in the web that Max Vilne had spun across the Atlantic.

"Amelia," Finn said, tapping at the keyboard with a rhythm that matched his train of thought, "I've been thinking. Richmond's transport business—it was the perfect Trojan horse for someone like Vilne."

"It seems like an unlikely route into the country," Amelia leaned back, her chair creaking under the shift of weight. Her eyes, sharp and seeking, met his. "You're sure he'd go through all that trouble rather than securing a fake passport on the black market?"

"Thomas Richmond didn't just have ships and logistics at his fingertips," Finn countered, his mind galloping through facts and figures. "He had trust. The kind of trust that gets you past customs without a second glance. And Vilne, he thrives on exploiting trust. It all fits. Vilne has been known to use people then kill them once he is done with them."

"Conveniently killing Richmond to cover his tracks, but..." Amelia trailed off, skepticism lingering in her voice.

"But nothing," Finn interjected, swiveling the chair to face her directly. "Max doesn't leave loose ends. That's what makes him so damned hard to pin down."

Amelia folded her arms, her brows furrowing as she processed Finn's words. "And what about the castle grounds? The early recon, the photographs... It doesn't fit. I mean, I don't know Vilne like you do, but he's a violent psychopath. I can't picture him skulking around with a camera days before a murder, snapping pictures."

"Ah," Finn said, a slow nod accompanying his realization that

Amelia hadn't seen this side of their adversary. "That's where you're wrong. Max Vilne is meticulous; he plans every step. Those photos are part of his game. He loves to draw out the plan. Taking those pictures let him know where to break in, but it went wrong. His violence comes after the preparation. It's cold, calculated."

"Calculated enough to mess up so badly and have to improvise the killing of the Richmonds?" Amelia challenged, her tone laced with doubt.

"No one's perfect," Finn leaned back, his shadow falling across the floor behind him. "Max is sending us a message. He wants us to know he's here and that he's always several moves ahead."

"Alright," Amelia conceded, pushing herself up from her chair, her eyes once again scanning the list of names. "Let's keep going. The sooner we find the connection, the sooner we can end this. We should keep looking at the email threats sent to Gregory Harding and the phone contacts Tanner gave us of his activist friends."

"Agreed," Finn murmured, his thoughts mirroring the relentless tick of the clock on the wall—a reminder that time was both ally and enemy in the hunt for Max Vilne.

Something now caught Finn's eye as he scrolled through several names. "Here." Finn's finger jabbed at the monitor, highlighting a name that stood out like a sore thumb amid the mundane. "Frank Butter."

"Seriously?" Amelia quirked an eyebrow, her lips twitching despite the gravity of their situation.

"Go ahead, laugh," Finn said with a half-smile, some tension easing from his shoulders. "Ridiculous name aside, the man has a record. Assault. Defended some ancient stones from a property developer with more muscle than sense. And he's on Boris Tanner's list of activist associates from his phone."

"Definitely sounds like our kind of suspect," Amelia noted dryly, her attention now fixed on Frank Butter's rap sheet.

"Wait a second..." Finn in leaned closer as he delved deeper into the file, his heart thudding with a sudden surge of adrenaline. The screen was reflected in his eyes, flickering with realization. "This guy had or has an SUV impounded on another occasion. He's since got it back."

"Tracks," Amelia murmured, catching on instantly. "Like the ones at Richmond Castle we found in the woods! I think we should pay Mr. Butter a visit."

"Let's hope he melts easily," Finn said as he pushed back from the desk, already reaching for his coat.

"Am I going to have to listen to numerous butter jokes for the duration?" Amelia asked with a knowing sigh.

"You better believe it," Finn answered.

"Dear Lord."

CHAPTER FOURTEEN

Finn felt a little uneasy, looking at the late night before him. The car's engine hummed a steady note as Finn navigated the winding roads that led to Frank Butter's last known residence. The landscape was a blur of green, but Amelia Winters stared through the passenger window with her thoughts seemingly as tangled as the overgrown hedgerows they passed.

"You know, Frank Butter might be our killer *and* have no connection to Vilne," Amelia's voice cut through the silence that had settled between them. "With Max Vilne out there, every second counts, and I can't shake the feeling we're running in the wrong direction."

Finn's grip on the steering wheel tightened, his jaw set in that determined way that told Amelia he saw something she didn't. "Max is cunning, but I think he might have slipped up this time. If Butter is one of his pawns, he could lead us right to him." His eyes never left the road as he drove, but his mind was clearly piecing together a puzzle only he could see.

"I want you to be right, Finn, but—" Amelia's words were abruptly interrupted by the shrill ring of Finn's phone. With a swift motion, he fished the device from his coat pocket and put it on speaker.

"Rob," Finn answered, keeping his tone level. "Shouldn't you be in your slippers by now?"

"Very good. I'm still at the constabulary. Got word you're off to see Frank Butter," Rob's voice came through, tinged with caution. "You do know who you're dealing with, right?"

"Should I be concerned?" Finn asked, stealing a glance at Amelia, who leaned in slightly to hear better.

"We've had dealings with him before during two other disputes. Frank's an ex-strongman contender," Rob informed, his tone suggesting this was no trivial detail. "In fact, he got close to the world title a few years ago."

"Great," Finn replied, the corner of his mouth lifting into a half-smile. " Have no fear, I once competed in the world's most handsome man competition, remember?"

Amelia snorted, her eyes rolling with the affectionate exasperation she reserved for Finn's ego. "You'd unquestionably take the crown in the world's most deluded man competition, Finn."

The tension broke, and a smirk played on Finn's lips, but his eyes remained focused on the journey ahead, a glint of the old agent sparked within them. Amelia shook her head, her own smirk hidden by the fall of her hair as she looked away.

"I'm just saying," Rob offered. "Be careful. Bring him back in one piece, would you, Winters?"

"No problem, Chief," Amelia said loudly. "Which piece would you like me to bring back?"

"Be careful, both of you. I'll send some backup, so do the sensible thing and wait before rushing in," Rob finished, and with a click, the call ended.

Finn eased the car around a sharp bend, the thicket giving way to an open field. He glanced at Amelia, catching the worry in her gaze. He understood it, felt it too. They were threading needles in the dark, hoping to catch on something solid.

"I don't think we need to worry about a strong man, we've faced much worse. We've got this," Finn said, more to convince himself than her.

"Rob is right," Amelia said. "I don't want to have to scrape you off the floor."

"The dance floor?" Finn asked.

"I'd make a bad pun about break dancing, but that seems to be your area of expertise," Amelia said. She looked at her phone, the GPS showing how close they were.

"Just around here, and that's us," she said, the lightheartedness receding away from her voice.

They pulled up outside a cottage, a quaint structure overshadowed by the mechanical graveyard that sprawled untamed around it. Engine blocks and rusted axles formed a metal moat, a barrier between them and whatever truths lay inside.

"Winters, do me a favor and wait here?"

"Why?" she asked.

"I have a feeling this Butter guy might not take kindly to being crowded," he said. "On his case file, it said he gets rowdy when confronted by several cops at once. Let me try."

"I don't think it's a good idea," Amelia said.

Finn grinned. "Trust me…"

"Okay, but I'll keep an eye on the car," she explained. "The first sign of trouble, I'm at your back."

"Here we go." Finn stepped out of the car, his movements deliberate, each step measured as he

navigated the detritus of abandoned automotive dreams. "What a lovely collection." Finn reached the door, his hand rapping against the wood in three solid thumps.

Finn turned and looked back at the car. He could see Amelia shifting in her seat and drumming her fingers on the dashboard. Finn gave her the OK sign with his hand.

As he turned around, the door swung open with a creak that seemed to groan from the depths of an ancient forest, revealing a human monolith. Frank Butter's silhouette filled the frame, dark and imposing against the light of his spartan living room. He was a titan clad in denim and flannel, muscles bulging even in repose.

"Hi, Frank Butter?" Finn asked.

"Who wants to know?" he asked in a deep voice.

"I'm Finn Wright, working with the Home Office and..."

"Whose in the car?" he said pointing past Finn to Amelia. "Are you police?"

"Well... Eh..." It was rare for Finn to feel any intimidation at the sight of another man, given his stature. This was one of those rare times.

"What's she doing?" Frank asked, pointing at her again.

She responded in kind and got out, probably knowing that Finn was in need of assistance, and walked up to where Finn and the mountain of a man were standing.

"Frank Butter? I'm Inspector Winters with the Hertfordshire constabulary," Amelia introduced herself crisply, stepping forward. "We need a moment of your time."

Frank's eyes were granite, cool and unyielding. "I don't do moments with the likes of you," he rumbled, his voice resonating like thunder rolling over hills.

"Two people are dead," Finn interjected, holding the giant's gaze with a steady, unflinching blue. "Lily and Thomas Richmond. Ring any bells?"

"Stew, Denny!" The bellow carried beyond the threshold, summoning forces hidden from view. Two figures emerged, each one as colossal as Frank, moving with the heavy certainty of landslide. They framed him now, three sentinels of flesh and bone.

"Leave now, or we'll have trouble," Frank warned, a tinge of anticipation coloring his words.

"Trouble isn't on our agenda today," Amelia countered, her tone even but edged with steel. "We want you to come with us for questioning."

"Arresting me?" There was a hint of amusement in Frank's voice, a challenge flickering in the depths of his steely gaze.

"No arrest—just a conversation," Amelia replied, her stance unwavering even as she assessed the trio before them with the tactician's eye of a chess master contemplating the board.

"Unless you've got evidence," Frank shot back, the corner of his mouth ticking up in a semblance of a smirk, "I think it's best you leave."

Amelia exchanged a glance with Finn, a silent exchange of resolve and intent. They wouldn't be deterred—not by size, nor by the veiled threats that hung in the air like the aftertaste of lightning.

"Frank," Finn began, his voice laced with a casualness that belied the tension simmering in the air, "you ever hear the fairy tale about the three giants who got outsmarted by a cunning little—"

"Save your breath," Frank's deep voice interrupted, the words rolling like thunder over the landscape of rusting car parts and creeping ivy. His expansive arms folded across his chest, a living barricade. The brothers behind him shifted, their heavy boots crunching on gravel.

Amelia peered at them through wary eyes. "We could do this the easy way, or—"

"Or what?" Stew rumbled, his eyebrow arching in a challenge.

"Or we find something else to bring you in for," Finn retorted, eyeing the assortment of vehicular detritus scattered around the cottage. He knew how to play the game; he'd danced this dance before, always one step ahead, even when the music turned sour.

"Like what?" Denny's voice was gruff, his stance aggressive. "You've got nothing on us."

"Public disturbance might suffice," Finn offered, the corner of his mouth twitching upward. "And I reckon some of these cars you've parked out here, half stripped, might not exactly have been acquired legitimately, am I right?"

"Thinks he's funny, does he?" Frank's face darkened. The air thickened with the scent of imminent violence, an electric current that buzzed against Finn's skin.

"Actually, I was a comedian in a former life," Finn said. "Would you like to hear a joke? It's a brilliant one. It involves the mother of three giants. Well, she's working the streets and..."

Without warning, Frank lunged forward, seizing a rusted car bumper from the ground. It whistled through the air, aimed squarely at Finn.

"Watch it!" Amelia cried out.

With reflexes honed from years in the field, Finn sidestepped, feeling the rush of air as the metal narrowly missed him. His fist shot out, connecting with Frank's midsection—a satisfying thud resonated, but the giant man merely absorbed the blow, unfazed.

"Is that all you've got, little man?" Frank sneered, his large hand reaching out.

"Apparently not," Finn muttered under his breath, the corner of his lips curling despite the situation. He knew well enough when brute force wouldn't cut it.

In a swift motion, Frank's hands clasped around Finn's torso, lifting him effortlessly into the air. Finn's feet dangled, his height advantage nullified. From this new vantage point, the world seemed smaller, the brothers' broad shoulders blotting out the weak autumn sun.

"Put me down, Frank," Finn said, surprisingly calm, even as he dangled like a puppet in the giant's grasp. "I can tell a different joke if you like."

"Do you ever shut up!" Frank growled, his grip tightening.

Finn exhaled slowly, his analytical mind racing through options. He needed to turn the tide, to shift the balance back into their favor. Amelia was already calculating her next move; he could see it in the set of her jaw, the determination in her eyes.

"Amelia," he called out, his voice steady, "care to assist?"

The brothers hesitated, a silent question passing between them. They were brutes but held onto some semblance of chivalry, outdated as it may be in the modern world.

"Assist with what, exactly?" Amelia asked, feigning innocence while her gaze swept the yard for something useful.

"Maybe a lesson in gravity," Finn suggested, still dangling from Frank's grip. "These gentlemen seem to have forgotten that what goes up must come down."

"Sorry, we don't hit ladies," one of the brothers grunted, his biceps bulging like melons under his shirt as he took a step back.

"Lucky me," Amelia quipped, sidestepping a rusty engine block and grasping a jagged piece of metal that looked like it had been part of a car door in a previous life. With a fluid motion born of years on the force, she swung it at Frank's exposed knee.

The impact resonated with a metallic clang, and Frank's face contorted not in pain but surprise as his hold faltered. Finn's feet found the ground with an unceremonious thump, and he couldn't resist, "The bigger they are, the harder they—"

"Fall," Amelia finished for him, dropping the twisted metal and smirking at the sight of Frank rubbing his knee.

Their brief moment of triumph was interrupted by the wail of sirens, and a police car skidded to a halt, gravel spitting out from its tires. Three constables poured out, their expressions caught between concern and bewilderment upon seeing Finn sprawled on the ground and Amelia standing triumphant.

"Should've waited for backup," Finn grumbled from his makeshift seat on the earth, dusting himself off with a sheepish grin. "But I think now we have a good reason to put Frank in cuffs and question him."

"Arrest these men," Amelia commanded, pointing at Frank Butter and his brothers.

"Assault on a handsome American and obstruction," Finn added, still catching his breath as he got to his feet. His mind was already cataloging the evidence they'd need to justify the charges.

The constables were quick to comply, though Frank towered over them like a mountain over saplings. Cuffs seemed absurdly small in his massive hands, yet he offered them without resistance, a knowing look in his eye that spoke volumes about his confidence.

"Right, let's get you to the station," Amelia said, her tone brooking no argument.

The journey to their car was a short one, but fitting Frank into the backseat proved impossible; his frame was simply too large, his shoulders brushing both sides of the door frame simultaneously.

"Constables," Finn called out, trying to suppress a smirk, "we're going to need transport. And not just any transport—a van, preferably a big one."

CHAPTER FIFTEEN

Finn was getting fed up with all the driving back and forth, he gripped the wheel hoping this would be his last journey on the case, and that Frank Butter would have something on Vilne.

The car came to a halt, its tires crunching on the freshly laid gravel of the constabulary's parking lot. The Hertfordshire Constabulary Headquarters was a towering edifice of brick and glass, standing sentinel over Garden City like an austere guardian of law and order. Finn Wright, his hands still feeling the vibration of the wheel, stepped out into the brisk air that carried the scent of rain and asphalt. Amelia Winters followed suit, her sharp eyes scanning the surroundings with the meticulous attention of a woman who had long since learned to expect the unexpected.

"Does Rob really need all these rooms?" Finn remarked, eyeing the HQ's imposing structure. It was as if the building itself dared wrongdoers to challenge it.

"Only for your ego," Amelia said, locking the car with a beep that echoed off the walls. Her tone was light, but her posture was all business—shoulders back, chin up, a detective through and through.

They hadn't taken more than a few steps when Chief Constable Rob Collins materialized from the revolving doors, the lines around his eyes crinkling in a grin that didn't reach his serious gaze.

"Finn," he greeted with a nod that spoke of mutual respect born from years of friendship and service. "Amelia. I'm glad you made it in one piece."

"Finn nearly ended up in several," Amelia offered.

"Rob," Finn returned, the familiarity in his voice belying the tension that knotted his shoulders. One didn't easily shake off the burdens he carried—the weight of a tarnished badge, the ghost of a love lost, and the whispers of a trial that still clawed at him. But Finn's way in the world was to joke his way out of a bad place. "I had that giant right where I wanted him."

"Word in the office is you had quite the tussle with Frank Butter," Rob said, his mouth quirking in a smile that hinted at the daily absurdities of their line of work.

Finn grinned. "Took care of business," he confirmed, the words clipped. Frank Butter was now one less thorn in their side, but there were always more to take his place.

"I hope you didn't goad the man into a fight just to get him here," Rob said sarcastically.

"Oh never," Finn added in his on sardonic tone.

"You did well, Finn," Rob then said softly.

Amelia cleared her throat, a pointed sound that drew a sideways glance from Finn. "With a little help from Amelia," he conceded, the corner of his mouth twitching upwards despite himself.

"A little help!?" Amelia's laugh was a burst of warmth in the icy air. "That's one way to put it."

"Okay, a lot," Finn admitted. Amelia's intuition had steered them right more times than he cared to count, and her bravery had matched his own, stride for stride.

"Let's get inside," Amelia said, her keen gaze shifting to the entrance. "We might just have caught our murderer."

And with that, they moved into the building, navigating its many brightly lit hallways and rooms.

Rob, with his hands tucked into the pockets of his unbuttoned overcoat, eyed them both, the lines around his eyes crinkling with a mixture of amusement and concern. "We've put Frank in an interview room," he mentioned casually as they ascended a set of stairs. "I hope you've got kryptonite cuffs on him," Finn joked.

"Kryptonite?" Rob's chuckle was dry. "Afraid we're fresh out. But he's secure enough." He paused, then added, "And no sightings of Vilne yet before you ask. I just hope your suspect can give us something."

Finn's jaw tightened at the mention of Max Vilne. "How's Demi?" he asked, attempting to keep his voice level.

"Safe, but she's on edge," replied Rob, casting a glance sharp enough to slice through Finn's stoic exterior. "You might want to give her a ring later. We've got a couple of constables with her at every moment."

The suggestion gnawed at Finn's insides, churning up a storm of guilt and unresolved feelings. "After the interview," he said tersely, pushing the unwelcome emotions down deep where they wouldn't interfere with the task at hand.

"Right," Rob nodded, looking a little less certain than usual about things. Finn could feel that his friend thought differently to him. That Rob felt Finn should be more in touch with Demi. "I'll keep you advised. Good luck." And with that, Rob disappeared back into the maze of corridors.

The remaining two detectives moved through the building's sterile corridors, their footsteps resonating against the linoleum floor. They passed uniformed officers and clerks buried in paperwork, each glance and nod a silent testament to the gravity of the day ahead. Amelia led the way to the elevator, pressing the button with a decisive thumb.

"Up we go then," she said, the doors sliding shut with a hush.

As the elevator hummed upwards, Finn's mind raced. The tight space seemed to contract further with each floor they ascended. And suddenly, he was aware of just how close Amelia was to him in that small space. And how her perfume made him feel like holding her and telling her how he felt.

Exiting onto the third floor, they navigated to the interview room, its door ajar. Inside, Frank Butter sat, his large frame dwarfing the metal chair he was cuffed to. Like Tanner before him, there was no lawyer present, just Frank and his simmering defiance.

"Surprised to see you without legal representation, Frank," Finn remarked, stepping into the room, his eyes never leaving the suspect.

"Lawyers," Frank spat contemptuously, "are part of what's wrong with society."

"Where have we heard that from?" Finn mused aloud, turning to Amelia with a wry smile that didn't reach his eyes. "Do you guys read from the same script?"

Frank looked confused.

The sterile scent of antiseptic mingled with the less distinguishable odors of a room that had seen countless confessions and denials. Finn's gaze swept over the bland walls, noting how the dull paint seemed to absorb rather than reflect the fluorescent light overhead. He took his seat across from Frank Butter, whose hands were cuffed securely to the table, his bullish neck strained as he leaned back in an attempt at nonchalance.

Amelia was already seated, her posture upright and professional, betraying no hint of the adrenaline Finn knew coursed through them both. She pressed the record button on the interview tape, the click resounding with finality in the air.

"Interview commencing at 9PM," Amelia's voice was crisp, each word enunciated clearly for the record. "Present are Inspector Amelia Winters, consulting detective Finn Wright, and Mr. Frank Butter."

"Why wouldn't you answer our questions back at your house,

Frank?" Finn's question sliced into the silence like a scalpel, precise and probing.

Frank's lips twisted into a wry smile. "Answering questions got me locked up before." His eyes, cold and guarded, flicked toward Finn. "And I wouldn't trust you as far as I could throw you, Wright."

"Wouldn't use that analogy, Mr. Butter," Amelia interjected with deceptive lightness, her eyes twinkling as she glanced at Finn. "Turns out, you could throw Finn quite far."

Finn offered her a rueful look, acknowledging the jibe. Amelia winked at him.

His thoughts briefly flitted to Demi, safe but shaken—Rob's words echoing in his mind. Guilt knotted in his stomach, but this was the job; focus now, personal calls later. Finn reeled his attention back to Frank, who was watching them with an unreadable expression.

"Is that so?" Frank's tone was mocking.

"Your distrust is noted," Finn said, leaning forward, elbows resting on the cold metal of the table. "But we're not here to toss each other about—we need answers, Frank."

"Answers you'll twist to charge me?" Frank challenged, his posture stiffening against the chair.

"Only interested in the truth," Finn countered, feeling the familiar tug of the investigative dance—the push and pull between what was said and unsaid.

"Truth," Frank scoffed, "is a slippery thing in the hands of the law."

"Then let's try to grasp it together," Amelia suggested, her voice steady as she steered the conversation. "Starting with where you were last night."

"None of your business," Frank scoffed.

"Lily and Thomas Richmond," she began, her voice echoing slightly in the sparse room, "they were found dead yesterday morning. Murdered."

Frank's face remained impassive, but there was a tightening around his eyes, a subtle shift that suggested he was more invested than he let on. The fluorescent light above flickered momentarily, casting an otherworldly glow over his features.

"Don't act like you're unaware of who they are," Finn added. "You're part of an activist group that was working to stop the Richmond's from renovating the castle. What I wonder is, was there any line you weren't willing to cross in that pursuit?"

"You're currently being held for assault," Amelia explained. "But if you don't open up, you could be spending the night with a murder charge hanging over you."

"Murder's a dirty business," he finally said, his voice low and gruff.

"Indeed," Finn chimed in, leaning back in his chair, the metal legs scraping against the linoleum floor with a high-pitched squeal. "But we're not here to wax philosophical about the nature of crime. We're here because there's a connection between you and the castle protests. Or at least, someone who shared your... fervent opinions about the renovations."

"Renovations?" Frank snorted, the sound echoing off the barren walls. "Is that what we're calling it now? They're tearing the soul out of our country, brick by historical brick. And for what? Some modern monstrosity? No respect for what matters." He pulled up his shirt arm and revealed a Union Jack tattoo on his forearm.

"Your love for history is well documented," Amelia remarked, her pen poised above the notepad, ready to capture his every word. "Tell us, Frank, what is it exactly that the Richmonds represent to you?"

"They're wiping away English history," he spat, his hands clenching into fists on the table. The cuffs around his wrists glinted under the harsh lighting. "It's not just stone and mortar—it's our identity. If we lose that, what are we left with?"

Finn watched Frank intently, noting the passion that ignited behind the man's eyes—a flame that seemed to consume all reason. "History is important," Finn conceded, his voice measured. "But murder isn't a reasonable protest. It can't bring back the past."

"Nor should it," Frank retorted, his voice rising. "People don't care anymore. They don't understand that history is who we are as a people! You erase that, and you erase us. We're making sure our people don't forget themselves."

Amelia tapped her pen against the pad, seemingly considering the weight of his words. She was silent for a moment, allowing the tension to build before speaking again. "Do you think that's worth killing for, Mr. Butter? Is that why you were at the castle last night?"

His nostrils flared, a bull catching the scent of red. "No," he ground out. "I respect the past, but I'm no murderer. And I wasn't there at the castle."

"Then help us understand," Finn urged, leaning forward. "Help us preserve *your* future by finding those responsible."

"Preserve *my* future..." Frank echoed, almost to himself, his gaze dropping to the table as if seeing it for the first time.

Amelia and Finn exchanged a glance, and Finn was aware they were on the cusp of something—whether it was a breakthrough or another wall to break down, only time would tell.

Finn's gaze never wavered from the man across the table. The steel-gray of Frank Butter's eyes seemed to reflect back the sterile light of the interview room, casting a pallor over his weathered face.

"It must hurt you that it was a couple of Americans doing this," Finn said, his words deliberate, probing for a crack in Frank's armor.

A slow smile crept across Frank's features, more a baring of teeth than any sign of mirth. "I hear your accent," he retorted, leaning back in his chair which creaked under the shift of his weight. "You're trying to make me angry, like your joke about my size back at the cottage. I won't fall for that again."

Finn shrugged his shoulders with a hint of a grin, less than innocently.

"I couldn't care less that they were American," Frank continued, crossing his arms defiantly. His cuffs clinked, a subtle reminder of his constrained state. "There are just as many people who have lived here all their lives who would gladly demolish our castles and stately homes and replace them with fast food restaurants. Money isn't everything."

"Is heritage?" Finn asked, though the question hung in the air, rhetorical and laden with implications.

Amelia decided to steer the conversation elsewhere, shifting her focus to another angle. She leaned forward, resting her elbows on the cold surface. "Have you ever heard of a man named Max Vilne?"

Frank's forehead crinkled as if the name brought an unpleasant taste to his mouth. "Know the name from the news," he grumbled. "Some killer on the loose from America." He shook his head and gave a dismissive gesture. "But I don't know him and wouldn't want anything to do with him. He's sick"

"Wouldn't you?" Finn pressed, his tone sharp as a scalpel. But he was beginning to feel frustration set in like a frost first thing in the morning.

"Look here—" Frank started, but Amelia cut through his indignation with a wave of her hand.

"Mr. Butter, a man like Vilne... he's not the type to seek permission before he uses someone," she said evenly. "Whether you wanted anything to do with him or not could be irrelevant."

Finn's mind raced, piecing together motives and opportunities, the intricate puzzle of human malice and deceit. He was acutely aware of the camera in the corner, the silent witness to their verbal dance. Every word spoken, every nuance, had to count. He was always wary of suspects performing for the cameras in case they were used against them at a later date.

"Frank," he said, his voice a low drawl, "a man with your... passion for history, savvy to the end. You'd recognize a predator when you see one, wouldn't you?"

"Predator?" Frank scoffed, but there was a new wariness in his eyes.

"Someone who uses your cause for his own ends," Finn clarified, his gaze piercing. "Someone who might hide behind the mask of the righteous to carry out his own twisted form of justice."

Frank's lips parted, then closed. He looked from Finn to Amelia, the former agent's implication clear as day. Frank Butter, for all his bluster, was no fool.

"Nobody rules me. Max Vilne is not my concern," he finally muttered, looking away.

"Maybe he should be," Amelia whispered, almost to herself, but loud enough for both men to hear.

The tension in the room coiled tighter, a spring waiting to snap. And in the charged silence that followed, the three of them—cop, agent, and suspect—were connected by the invisible threads of a dark tapestry yet to be fully unveiled.

Finn narrowed his eyes, studying the man cuffed to the metal table. He needed to use the man's own history against him. "Frank, with your history of assaulting a landowner—"

"History?" Frank's voice cut through, sharp and unyielding as flint. "What you call history, I call being stitched up by those with deeper pockets. Enough of this! Last night, when your so-called murder happened, I was at an arm-wrestling contest. After that, a lock-in at The Black Swan."

"Lock-in?" Finn echoed, skepticism threading his tone.

"Yeap, lock-in," Frank said, a smirk tugging at his lips. "And before you ask, no, they weren't all card-carrying members of my 'Save Our Heritage' group."

"Arm wrestling and ale," Finn mused aloud, though his thoughts were racing. Could a behemoth like Frank really have been content with mere pub games while a storm brewed outside? He glanced at Amelia, her pen paused above her notepad. He could see she was considering something.

The knock on the door was abrupt, a staccato rhythm that jarred the room's tense atmosphere. Rob Collins now appeared, poked his head through the gap, his usual composure edged with urgency. "Finn, Amelia, can you step outside for a moment?"

"Excuse us, Frank," Amelia said, her voice cool as she stopped the tape and rose from her chair.

Outside, the corridor felt too narrow, the air too stale. Finn sensed Amelia's shift in posture, the steel in her spine as she faced Rob.

"Chief, could you have someone look into the suspect's alibi?" Amelia said. "He says he was at an arm wrestling competition at The Black Swan and there are plenty of witnesses."

"Sure... But... Amelia, there's been an incident." Rob's words were clipped, his gaze fixed on her. "I'm so sorry, but... Your flat... There's been a fire. Burned down, apparently."

The blood drained from Amelia's face, her skin suddenly ashen. For a moment, Finn saw vulnerability flicker in her eyes before she masked it with the stoicism he'd come to admire. "Burned down?" Her voice was almost disbelieving, a crack in her professional veneer.

"Arson, we suspect," Rob continued. "I'm sorry, Amelia."

"Any... any leads on who did it?" There was a tremor in her query, a personal affront mingling with the detective's need for answers.

"Too early to say," Rob replied. "But with the break-in at the cottage before and the dolls that looked like you, me, and Demi, I think we can conclude it might have been Max Vilne."

Finn watched as Amelia absorbed the blow, her fists clenching momentarily at her sides. He knew her life, those fragments of normalcy away from the job, had just turned to ash. It was a vulnerability he understood all too well—a reminder that the chaos they sought to tame could reach out and engulf their own worlds in flames.

"Are you okay?" Finn asked softly, gently touching her shoulder.

"Let's go," Amelia said abruptly, her tone leaving no room for argument. She brushed past Rob, determination etched into every line of her body. Finn followed suit, his own thoughts churning with the realization that this fire was more than an act of destruction; it was a message, and they were meant to read it loud and clear.

CHAPTER SIXTEEN

Finn could smell it from half a mile away. The scent of charred memories hung thick in the air as he parked at an awkward angle on the curb. Greenbridge's narrow streets were clogged with emergency vehicles, their lights painting the dusk with urgent hues of blue and red. His gaze climbed three stories of the apartment building, where smoke still whispered secrets from Amelia's windows, though the fire brigade's hoses lay slack, spent from battle.

"Damn," Finn muttered, squinting through the windshield at the soot-streaked facade.

Amelia sat motionless beside him, her normally composed features drawn taut with silent anguish. Her eyes—sharp tools that had dissected countless crime scenes—now reflected a personal horror. Finn could see it. This was her sanctuary violated, her private world made public spectacle.

"Amelia," Finn said gently, his voice crackling like the dying embers they both could smell, "maybe we should hang back until they're done."

"No." The word slashed the air between them, quick and decisive. She flung open the car door, and the noise of the scene rushed in—the murmur of bystanders, the authoritative shouts of firefighters coordinating their efforts, the distant wail of an ambulance retreating from the chaos.

Stepping onto the pavement, she smoothed back a stray lock of hair that had escaped her otherwise neat bun and straightened her jacket with a tug—the armor of Inspector Winters snapping into place.

"Can't wait," she said with urgency lacing her words. "It's my home."

Finn watched as she approached the nearest firefighter, a man still wearing his helmet, ash smeared across his yellow coat like war paint. Amelia fished out her ID, presenting it with a hand that betrayed no tremor.

"Inspector Winters," she announced, her voice carrying authority even in its strain. "I need to see it."

The firefighter hesitated, his gaze shifting from the ID to the smoldering building, but Amelia's stare held him as effectively as handcuffs. With a curt nod, he stepped aside, granting passage.

Without looking back at Finn, Amelia crossed the threshold, stepping over a hose as limp as a discarded snake. The entrance gaped wide, a portal to a gutted realm where once there had been life, laughter, and the mundane comfort of the everyday.

"Wait!" Finn called after her, his own instincts lurching him forward. He knew protocol, the sanctity of a crime scene—even one still cooling—but this was different. This was Amelia, and if the flames hadn't already consumed her possessions, then surely this violation would sear her soul.

He jogged to catch up, his shoes crunching on debris that spilled from the building's wounded belly. A sooty taste settled on his tongue, the bitter tang of destruction mingling with the coppery hint of adrenaline that now surged through him.

"Everything will be okay," he murmured more to himself than to the receding figure of Amelia ascending the staircase before him. It was a promise hanging in the smoky air, fragile as ash, yet delivered with the conviction of a man who'd spent his life chasing certainty in a world mired by shadows and doubt.

And as the sirens wailed their mournful song into the encroaching night, Finn Wright followed where Amelia Winters led, into the heart of the smoldering unknown.

The charred remnants of the doorway loomed as a grim sentinel against the twilight sky outside. Finn's resolve hardened like the cooling embers around him, his gaze arrowing to the staircase that Amelia had taken. It was then that a solid hand landed on his chest, halting him—a firefighter, his face obscured by soot and the shield of his helmet.

"Sorry, mate, you can't go in there," the firefighter said, voice muffled but firm.

Finn glanced at the embroidered badge over the man's heart, noting the emblem of Greenbridge Fire Department. "I'm with her—Inspector Winters." He gestured vaguely upward, towards Amelia's vanished form. "I need to make sure she's safe."

"Without ID? No way," the second firefighter chimed in, stepping beside his colleague. His stance mirrored an unspoken solidarity, a wall Finn had to breach.

"Ever heard of that American detective?" Finn asked, a tinge of urgency lacing his words. "The one they've been talking about all over the news?"

"American detective?" The first firefighter tilted his head slightly, curiosity piqued.

"Yeah, the American FBI agent lending a hand with the homicides here in the UK? Supposed to be quite the looker, too," Finn added with a wry half-smile pulling at the corner of his mouth.

"Ah, I think I know who you mean," the second firefighter said, scratching the back of his neck beneath the rim of his helmet. "Got a name?"

"Finn Wright," he announced, assuming the pose from the newspaper article—the one where he appeared in deep contemplation, fingers brushing his chin, eyes narrowed in thought. It was part theatrics, part earnest appeal.

"Let me get a good look at you," the first firefighter squinted, scrutinizing Finn's features. A beat passed, laden with the tension of recognition.

"Alright, Finn Wright. Go ahead," he relented, stepping aside with a nod that carried the weight of reluctant respect.

"Thanks," Finn breathed out, relief threading through the gratitude. As he moved past the firefighters, their radios crackled with updates, a sonic backdrop to the tragedy unfolding.

Inside, the air hung heavy with the scent of ruin. Each step on the staircase was a silent testament to the chaos that had raged within these walls. Finn ascended with purpose, the pulse of his mission thrumming in his veins. He could almost feel the heat of the fire that had licked its way across the room of an inspector who'd swiftly become more than just a partner to him.

Amelia needed him. That single thought cleaved through the fog of smoke, honing his focus to a razor's edge. Whatever awaited them in the remnants of her life, they would confront it together. Finn Wright didn't just chase after truths hidden in shadows—he chased after those he deemed his responsibility.

"Amelia," he whispered, the name bolstering his stride as he reached the landing. Ahead lay the charred skeleton of what once was a sanctuary, now laid bare for all to see. Finn steeled himself for the sight of devastation, ready to offer whatever solace he could muster in the face of such loss.

Finn's boots clapped an urgent rhythm against the stairs as he ascended to the third floor, the air growing more acrid with each flight. His lungs protested the residual fumes, but the sound of muffled weeping propelled him forward, eclipsing his discomfort.

"Amelia!" he called out as he reached her apartment, the door a blackened void in an otherwise orderly hallway.

The room beyond was a desolate landscape, shadows clinging to the scorched walls where memories had once flourished. Finn's eyes darted across the devastation, finally settling on Amelia's silhouette, her figure a stark contrast amid the charred remains of her living room. Firefighters moved like specters in the background, their presence a grim reminder of the day's events.

"Everything... I've lost everything," Amelia's voice broke through the silence, barely above a whisper.

Finn closed the distance between them in swift strides. "Amelia," he said softly, reaching out to envelop her in a protective embrace.

She leaned into him, her body trembling as if she might crumble without his support. Finn could feel the fight in her, the resilience that made her an exceptional inspector, now momentarily eclipsed by vulnerability.

"I'm here," he murmured, his hand finding its way to her hair, fingers brushing away soot and sorrow with equal tenderness. "We'll get through this."

The faint crackle of a firefighter's radio punctuated the moment, a subtle reminder of the peril that had passed—and the dangers that might still lurk. Finn's gaze swept the room, taking in every detail, the gears of his analytical mind already turning. He wasn't just here to console; he was here to find answers.

"Okay?" he asked, pulling back slightly to look into her eyes, seeking confirmation that she was ready to stand with him against the looming threat.

Amelia nodded, a fragile determination settling over her features. "Okay."

With the quiet resolve that had come to define their partnership, they stepped back from the edge of despair and toward the unknown dangers ahead. There was work to be done, and neither fire nor foe would deter them from seeking justice.

Finn watched his partner intently as Amelia's eyes found the firefighter's boots first, coated in a film of ash as they approached through the detritus of her living room. The soles left imprints on the charred carpet, temporary marks that were nothing compared to the permanent scars the fire had etched into her life.

"Inspector Winters?" The firefighter's voice was gentle amid the crackling remnants of her sanctuary.

Amelia glanced up, to the reflective visor and and eyes that Finn felt held concern but not the answers his partner sought.

"I'm... I'll manage," she replied, her voice steadier than she felt, wiping away the tears that betrayed her stoicism.

"Any idea how this got started?" Finn asked, motioning towards an evidence bag that another firefighter was carefully sealing.

"Tell me it's not what it looks like," Amelia said, her gaze fixating on the bag with a grim intuition.

"Can't be certain until the lab results come back, but..." The firefighter's hesitation confirmed her fears before his words did. "Looks deliberate. Found remnants of paper, soaked in what seems like an accelerant, probably petrol, in the bedroom."

The word 'deliberat' seemed to change Amelia's demeanor. Finn imagined that it echoed in Amelia's mind, a sinister whisper that stirred the embers of suspicion she harbored.

"Anyone you can think of who'd do this?" The firefighter's question hung heavy in the air, weighted with implications that Finn wished Amelia could ignore. But he knew they could not ignore what that fire *meant*.

She turned to Finn, who had been watching the exchange with hawk-like intensity. His jaw set, a telltale sign of his resolve hardening. "Max Vilne," he stated, the name falling like a gavel, marking both accusation and verdict.

"Vilne..." Amelia's own voice sounded distant. To Finn, it was as if she didn't know how to respond to what had happened—her home, her refuge, now reduced to ruins by a ghost from their shared past.

Finn felt a rage building in his bones that he hadn't felt for an age. How dare he attack Amelia's life like that. He could feel his blood boiling, but he knew that the most important thing he could do was not let the anger overcome him into making mistakes – but to keep Amelia safe at all costs.

"Greenbridge has a hotel, right?" Finn's practicality cut through the haze of her shock, a lifeline thrown into turbulent waters.

"Yes, the Queen's Arms, near the market square," she answered almost automatically. Amelia gazed at the remnants around her as if her mind were already cataloging what needed to be salvaged, which leads to pursue.

"Let's get a couple of rooms there. Regroup." Finn's suggestion was more than just strategy; it was solidarity.

"I can't have you involved more than you already are. Go back to your cottage, Finn," Amelia argued.

Finn could see something he had rarely seen in her eyes before – fear. Despite her words, it was as though the thought of solitude in the wake of such violation chilled her more than the evening air seeping through the broken windows ever could.

"No chance," Finn countered, his tone brooking no argument. "Not when that psychopath is taking the game to this level. I'm worried for your safety."

Finn was glad to see a look on her face, an appreciation. He hoped that his words wrapped around her like the coat she no longer owned, offering a semblance of security amid her loss. He could see it all inside of her. It wasn't just her apartment that had been torched—it was her sense of normalcy, her belief in a place she could control. Now, all she could do was watch the remains smolder, knowing that somewhere out there, Max Vilne was plotting his next move.

Something then slowly changed in her expression, as though she were now accepting of the situation.

"There's nothing left," she said, almost sobbing.

Finn put his arm around her shoulders, gently moving her away from the horror of it all.

"There's nothing left to do here, let the firefighters do their job, and we'll do ours," he said, softly.

The acrid scent of charred memories lingered in the air as Finn and Amelia stepped out into the cool night. The building behind them, a blackened shell against the darkening sky, seemed to loom over them—a grim sentinel bearing witness to the night's events.

"Come on," Finn urged, guiding her with a gentle hand at the small of her back. "Let's get away from here."

Amelia nodded, wiping a tear from her eye. The orange glow of street lamps cast long shadows that danced around them, as if Max Vilne's presence was an invisible specter haunting their every move, and Finn feared that he was capable of bringing more tears to the world than anyone he had ever encountered.

"Where is this hotel?" Finn asked, his eyes scanning the quiet streets of Greenbridge, alert for any sign of danger.

"Two streets down, on Harper Street, just off Market Square," Amelia replied, her voice carrying a determination that belied the tremor beneath it. She could looked at Finn as though the weight of his gaze on her, protective and unwavering. He hoped that it served as a reminder that she wasn't alone.

"Good. Once we're there, we'll have more eyes around us." Finn's tone was resolute, but there was an undercurrent of concern that didn't escape Amelia. "If Max Vilne even thinks about following us, he won't find it so easy to strike without witnesses."

"Is that supposed to make me feel better?" Amelia quipped, though the attempt at lightness fell flat. Her shoes clicked against the concrete, hollow against the silence enveloping the town.

"After today, it's not about feeling better. It's about staying alive," Finn said solemnly. Deep down, however, all Finn could feel was a burning desire for revenge, a need to make him pay for what he had done to Amelia.

CHAPTER SEVENTEEN

Finn felt exhausted from the day's investigation, but while he wanted to sleep, he couldn't leave Amelia's side. The Greenbridge hotel emerged like a quaint portrait from the drizzle, its warm golden glow spilling out onto the slick cobblestone street. After parking nearby, Finn walked quietly with Amelia to its entrance.

As Finn Wright pushed open the heavy oak door, the foyer's intimate charm enveloped him and Inspector Amelia Winters in an almost tangible embrace. The lobby was adorned with vintage floral wallpaper and dark wood paneling that whispered tales of a bygone era, while a small fire crackled invitingly in the hearth.

"Evening," Finn greeted the receptionist, a middle-aged woman with a beehive hairdo that defied gravity. Her nameplate declared her as 'Sylvia.'

"Good evening, sir, ma'am. How may I assist you?" Sylvia's voice was infused with a practiced cheeriness.

"We need two rooms for the night," Finn said, glancing at Amelia, whose keen eyes surveyed the space with a detective's thoroughness.

"Of course, just one double room then?" Sylvia's fingers hovered over the keyboard, poised to seal their fate.

Amelia's brow arched elegantly, and Finn's ears reddened as he hastily corrected, "No, no, separate rooms, please."

"Ah, my apologies!" Sylvia chuckled, her earrings jangling like chimes. "I sometimes jump to conclusions. Been watching too many of those romantic dramas on telly, I suppose."

"Understandable mistake," Amelia offered with a wry smile, her tone teetering between amusement and professionalism. But Finn knew Amelia so well that he could see past that. She was clearly trying to be brave, but underneath she was adrift in a sea of sadness from the day's events.

"Though, considering our day, romance is the last thing on our minds," Finn added, trying to infuse humor into his voice to dispel the awkward air. He caught Amelia's eye, and they shared a fleeting look of camaraderie.

"Right you are, sir! One room for you, Mr...?"

"Wright. Finn Wright."

"And for you, Miss?"

"Winters. Amelia Winters."

"Very well," Sylvia typed away briskly, her nails tapping a staccato rhythm against the keys. "Here are your keys. Room 204 for you, Mr. Wright, and 206 for you, Miss Winters. Just up the stairs and to your left."

"Thank you," Amelia said, accepting her key with a nod. Finn took his own, feeling the solid weight of the metal tag in his palm.

"Hope you find our little hotel comfortable," Sylvia said, beaming at them.

"Looks charming," Finn replied genuinely, allowing himself a moment to appreciate the cozy atmosphere despite the turmoil that had led them here.

"Charm's one thing we have in abundance," Sylvia agreed, her voice trailing off as Finn turned toward the staircase, Amelia in step beside him.

As they ascended, the plush carpet muffled their footsteps, and Finn couldn't help but think how this place seemed a world away from the chaos swirling around their investigation. But chaos, he knew, had a way of seeping through the cracks of even the most serene facades.

The keys, cool and metallic, settled into Finn's hand with a definitive click as Sylvia, the receptionist, slid them across the polished wood surface. The mundane transaction was disrupted by the shrill chime of his mobile phone vibrating in his jacket pocket. Finn glanced at the screen, the name 'Demi' igniting a complex knot of emotions within him.

"Go on," Amelia urged, her tone light despite the weight of exhaustion pressing upon her features. "I'm just going to crash for a bit." She stifled a yawn with the back of her hand, her eyes reflecting understanding and something that might have been concern.

"Alright," he said, thumbing the answer button. He turned slightly away, instinctively seeking privacy in the open foyer.

"Hello?"

"Finn?" Demi's voice was fraught with tension, a tremor betraying her usual poise. "Have you seen the news?"

"Slow down, Demi." Finn steadied his voice, an effort to project calm. "What's happened?"

"Your partner—Amelia's apartment—it's been set on fire."

Finn's mind returned to the images of blackened walls of Amelia's flat flickering behind his eyes. "I know... She's okay. It's just been a bit of a shock."

"Was it Vilne? It's all over the news here, but they didn't mention his name. I'm worried, Finn," Demi said, her voice wavering.

"You're safe, Demi," Finn felt his jaw clench, the molten anger forging a steely resolve. "We're all safe at the moment. I will catch him, and we can put it behind us."

"Safe... but for how long?" Her words hung between them like a specter, the unspoken fears for their safety amplifying the distance of the phone line.

"Look, Demi, I—" Finn started, but he cut himself off, acutely aware of Amelia's presence nearby. She had paused halfway up the stairs and was looking back at him, her expression unreadable.

"Are you okay?" he asked after a pause, changing tack.

"Shouldn't I be asking you that? You're the one in the middle of all this."

"Occupational hazard," he quipped weakly, though humor was far from his heart. "But I'm managing. Where are you right now?"

"Safe house, two constables," she said, her words clipped, efficient, but Finn heard the undercurrent of fear. He imagined the stark white walls of her temporary sanctuary, the way her gaze must flit to the window at every passing shadow.

"Good. Stay put for now," he instructed, though the notion of her being truly safe while Max Vilne roamed free seemed like a fool's hope.

Deep down, something pulled at his nerves.

Send her home, he thought for a moment. But would be any safer in the States from Vilne's reach? And what would it mean for them? Demi had been adamant that she wouldn't leave the UK without him by her side, that she had come there to renew their relationship. Finn was so confused as to his feelings for her. Was that what he truly wanted?

"Where are you holed up?" Demi's inquiry came quick, tinged with an edge that suggested a thousand unspoken accusations.

"Greenbridge," he replied, breaking from his thoughts, watching as the receptionist shuffled papers, oblivious to the gravity of their conversation. "The hotel has a cozy foyer, not unlike—"

"Isn't that where Amelia's flat burned down?" Demi interrupted, the question sharp, pointed.

The same town, yes." His response was curt, eyes tracing the intricate pattern of the carpet as if it held answers.

"Amelia..." She drew out the name, letting it hang between them like a specter. "You're close to her."

"Amelia is a colleague and a friend," he asserted, feeling the need to reinforce boundaries that had become blurred by circumstance. "My room is my own."

"Of course," she said, but the skepticism in her tone was palpable, like the hum of electricity before a storm.

"Nothing's changed, Demi." Finn straightened, the receiver cool and impersonal against his warming skin. "Not in that regard. I still don't know where we stand, if we stand at all."

"Right," she sighed, and he could picture her running a hand through her hair, a gesture of frustration he knew all too well. There was a vulnerability in Demi's voice that struck a chord in him, one that resonated with memories of what they once shared.

There was a silence between them, and Finn was struggling to know what to say.

"So... Greenbridge?" Demi's voice filtered through the phone, tinged with curiosity. "What's it like there?"

Finn glanced out of the large window in his room, taking in the quiet hum of the small town at night. "It's quaint," he replied, watching an elderly couple amble past a row of shops. "Small, not that different from a hundred others."

"Doesn't sound like there's much to see," came her almost indifferent observation.

His gaze shifted to the castle in the distance, a silhouette against the dusking sky. "No, not much for sightseeing." Lightning struck through his mind. The words tugged at the hem of his thoughts, unraveling a theory as swift and as sure as any storm. *The man with the camera at Richmond Castle– could he have been from out of town?* His mind began to thrum with the implications.

"Are you still there, Finn?"

"Sorry," he said, "just thinking about the case." He could almost feel the neural pathways firing, connecting dots that had previously seemed disparate.

"Anything I should know about?" There was a note of concern in her voice now.

"Maybe," he murmured, and as he did, the image of the photographer crystallized into something ominous. Finn's pulse quickened—not from fear but from the prospect of a breakthrough. Not locals, but a tourist?

"Listen, Demi, I've got to run," he cut in, already turning towards the staircase.

"I understand," she said, sounding as though she didn't quite accept his need to leave the conversation. "Please look after yourself." *That* she did clearly mean.

"Always do," he replied, though the promise tasted like ash in his mouth. "I've got to go, Demi. We'll talk later. But call if you need anything."

"Okay... Bye, Finn."

"Goodbye, Demi."

He ended the call and slipped the phone back into his pocket, feeling its weight like a stone. But something had clicked in his mind, and he had to tell Amelia about it right away.

CHAPTER EIGHTEEN

Finn approached the nondescript hotel door, its peeling paint a silent witness to countless transient lives that passed through. He rapped his knuckles against the wood, a staccato beat that cut through the hush of the corridor. A voice from within, muffled by the barrier, called out with an edge of caution.

"Who is it?"

"Amelia, it's Finn," he replied, leaning slightly closer to the door as if proximity would offer more reassurance than his words.

The sound of locks disengaging preceded the door swinging open. Amelia stood in the threshold, swathed in an over sized white bathroom robe that enveloped her frame, her damp hair framing her face like tendrils of nightshade. The plush fabric swallowed her whole, and for a moment, Finn's grim thoughts were punctured by the absurdity of the image before him.

"Blimey, you look like a displaced polar bear," he quipped, a lopsided grin momentarily easing the lines of concern etched into his face.

Amelia rolled her eyes but couldn't suppress a small smirk, a fleeting respite from the gravity that clung to them both like the early morning fog outside. "Fashion advice from a man who wears the same two sets of clothes on rotation? I'll take my chances, thanks."

She stepped aside, allowing him entry, the warmth from the room spilling onto the corridor's cold tiles. As Finn crossed the threshold, the space between them seemed to shrink, charged with an unspoken energy. It was a dance they had become accustomed to—this delicate interplay of camaraderie shadowed by the weight of unsolved mysteries and veiled intentions.

He brushed past her, noting how the aroma of jasmine mingled with the sterile scent of the hotel soap—a peculiar combination that somehow suited Amelia. It was these small details he found himself cataloging, pieces of her that he might later assemble into something resembling understanding.

Finn glanced back at her, taking in the weary resolve that set her jaw firm and narrowed her gaze. They were two sides of the same coin, worn yet unyielding, each turn of fate pushing them closer, not just in proximity, but in purpose.

Finn observed Amelia, the way she held herself tightly within the plush robe as if it were armor against the world outside. He cleared his throat softly, a prelude to the question he almost dreaded to ask. "Are you... okay?"

Amelia's gaze drifted past him, focusing on some indistinct point in the room. "It's surreal," she finally said, her voice carrying a hollow timbre. "To have everything tangible that made up your life just... vanish. I don't know how long it'll take to process."

"Insurance?" Finn prodded gently, not wanting to pry yet feeling the need to understand the scope of her loss.

"Sure," she sighed, "but it's the sentimental things, isn't it? The ones insurance can't bring back."

In that instant, a connection sparked in Finn's mind like a neuron firing after a long silence. "The things from your apartment..." he began hesitantly, "were there any that belonged to your deceased fiancé?"

Amelia's nod was small, almost imperceptible, but it carried the weight of unshed tears and memories best left untouched. "Yes."

"I'm so sorry," he murmured, the words feeling inadequate for the depth of her loss.

A sharp exhale escaped her, and Amelia's eyes met his squarely, a spark of something indefinable flickering within them. "Thank you, Finn. But you didn't come here to talk about the fire, did you?"

He hesitated, caught off-guard by her perceptiveness. It was this intuition that made her an outstanding detective, the same intuition that had woven their paths together in this tangle of suspicion and urgency.

"No," he admitted, his resolve refocusing like a lens sharpening an image. "No, I didn't."

Finn paced the length of Amelia's hotel room, a space adorned with the sterile charm typical of such establishments. The beige walls bore generic prints of pastoral England, and the only personal touch was Amelia's laptop open on a desk, its screen an island of blue light in the dimness.

"Amelia," he began, pausing mid-stride, "I've been ruminating on something." He turned to face her, noting the way she wrapped the plush robe tighter around herself, as if bracing for an unwelcome chill. "The man who was seen taking photographs outside the Richmond estate days before the murders... What if he's not an angry local or a local activist? Someone like a tourist."

"A tourist?" Her brows furrowed, skepticism etched into her features.

"*Like* a tourist," Finn affirmed, his hands animated as he spoke. "It might not be someone within our immediate circle of suspects – not a local or anyone from the activist group. It could be someone who has come to the area temporarily."

Amelia leaned back against the headboard, the fluffy texture of the robe contrasting with the sharp alertness in her eyes. "That could potentially rule out Max Vilne," she mused aloud, her voice steady but tinged with doubt.

"Potentially," Finn conceded, "but we both know Vilne's reach isn't limited to locals. He could easily manipulate a tourist, use them as a pawn."

"True," she acknowledged, her gaze locked onto his. "Vilne has the means and the cunning to orchestrate that kind of deception."

"Right," Finn replied, feeling the familiar surge of adrenaline that came with the chase. His mind whirred with possibilities, each more menacing than the last. Max Vilne was a shadow they had yet to catch, always looming just beyond their grasp.

"Then again..." Amelia's voice trailed off, her eyes narrowing in thought. "A tourist wouldn't have the same vested interest in the outcome. Why would they risk it?"

"Money," Finn suggested bluntly, "or maybe they were promised something more. We can't underestimate Vilne's capability to exploit weaknesses."

"Or perhaps," Amelia said, rising to her feet, her movements fluid and determined, "we're dealing with someone who simply enjoys the game. Someone who craves the thrill of being involved, even tangentially."

"Could be," Finn admitted, the idea unsettling yet plausible. "And if that's the case, we need to act fast before they disappear back into obscurity."

Amelia nodded, her expression hardening with resolve. "We'll need to widen our net, consider every fleeting presence around the time of the murder. That's one hell of a task."

"Agreed." Finn's pulse quickened, his thoughts racing ahead. They were stepping into uncharted territory, leaving the safety of tested theories behind. But it was a necessary gambit and one he was willing to take with Amelia by his side. "But I also wonder if there was a reason for the photographs beyond the murder.

"What do you mean?" Amelia asked.

"I'm not sure yet," he said. "But in the back of my mind, I feel like there's something else here. That the murders may have been almost a secondary goal. Whoever took the photos, whoever killed the Richmonds—if they are indeed the same person—maybe there was something that they wanted at the castle. I'm trying to think why Vilne would potentially scout out the place. What was he looking for? It's probably likely that he killed them after getting what he wanted. That's how twisted he is."

"Let's revisit the evidence," Amelia proposed, "see if there are any traces, anything overlooked that might connect back to this hypothetical tourist."

"Let's do it," Finn agreed, a sense of unity between them as palpable as the tension in the air. Together, they'd peel back the layers of deceit, inching ever closer to the truth lurking beneath.

In the suffused glow of the hotel room's bedside lamp, Amelia's eyes were a sharp contrast to the softness around them. Finn caught a glint of something indefinable within their depths as she leaned forward, her fingers swiping deftly across her phone screen.

"Let's take another look at those emails the estate agent showed us," Amelia suggested, her voice cutting through the hum of the air conditioning unit. "There might be something we missed. We ended up being so caught up with the Tanner list of activists and Frank Butter, that there could be something in the threatening emails sent to the real estate agent."

"Good idea," Finn replied, his mind snapping back into focus. "Gregory Harding was convinced that we'd find something there."

He shifted on the bed, their knees brushing accidentally under the weight of shared purpose. The proximity was a jolt to his senses, but he masked it with a nod towards Amelia's phone.

They settled into an unspoken rhythm, scrolling through the barrage of digital vitriol that had bombarded the real estate agent's inbox. Each message seemed more volatile than the last, rife with animosity towards the planned renovations of Richmond Castle.

"Most of these are just empty threats, keyboard warriors who wouldn't dare say any of this in person," Finn mused aloud, though his analytical gaze never left the screen.

"True, but amongst the chaff, there could be the seed of genuine intent," Amelia countered, her brows knitting together in concentration. "We should take them all seriously. I just hope one of them stands out as more concrete."

"Oh, and I meant to ask," Amelia said. "Can I borrow your phone charger later, I think mine went with everything at my flat."

Finn was hit by an unexpected and disarming urge to bridge the distance between them, to comfort her in some small way. His thoughts danced dangerously close to action; the warmth emanating from Amelia's skin was tantalizing, palpable even in the coolness of the room.

"Look at this," Amelia interrupted his internal tug-of-war, tapping at an email chain. The sender's name was Arron Reinhardt

"Arron Reinhardt.." Finn repeated, rolling the name around his tongue like a new taste, unfamiliar yet intriguing.

"His tone starts off almost...respectful," Amelia observed, scrolling through the initial pleasantries. "But then, here—" She stopped at a particular message, and Finn leaned closer to read over her shoulder.

"'I will be visiting your lovely town soon,'" Finn read aloud. "'And I truly hope to convince the Richmonds to reconsider their plans for the castle. I can be persuasive.'" He raised an eyebrow, looking to Amelia for her take.

"It's subtle, isn't it?" Amelia said, her voice laced with a newfound edge of excitement. "Not overtly threatening, but there's a clear implication there. He wanted to change their minds."

"Sounds like he had a vested interest in keeping the castle untouched," Finn added, running a hand through his hair. His thoughts churned with possibilities, assembling and reassembling scenarios like puzzle pieces.

"An interest strong enough to kill for?" Amelia pondered out loud, her detective's mind piecing together the potential implications. Finn watched her, admiring the relentless drive behind her questions.

"Maybe," he conceded, feeling the weight of the word hang between them. "We need to find out more about this Arron Reinhardt"

"Definitely," Amelia agreed, her thumb hovering over the screen as if hesitant to delve deeper into Reinhardt's words. Finn knew they were both aware that pulling on this thread could unravel something far larger than they anticipated.

"Could he be our tourist killer?" Finn wondered, not just to Amelia but also voicing the question silently to himself. As they sat there, side by side on the precipice of discovery, the unsaid truth lingered – they were no longer merely chasing a shadow; they were stepping into the lair of a potentially deadly adversary.

"Here's what I have on him," Amelia said, speaking and reading ahead at the same time. "Looks like he's a millionaire, an antiques dealer... But while I don't have a list of charges, it seems he's been investigated once before by the FBI for potentially selling stolen artifacts. Looks like the charges didn't stick."

"Okay," Finn mused out loud. "Let's say Arron Reinhardt has made his fortune from selling off antiques to the highest bidder. Doubling as some sort of activist wanting to 'preserve' history, he could get access to places and relics, steal them, then sell them on the black market. Let's say he normally scouts out a place, which would make him the photographer who was spotted days before the murders. Then, he breaks in and things go wrong. The murder weapon could even have been what he came for."

"So, no Vilne, and no pre-meditated murders?" Amelia asked.

"I know Vilne's got a connection to this case," Finn said, his voice filled with frustration. "But he could simply have pulled the strings. He has previous for manipulation, psychological extortion. He could have set the thing up somehow."

"Finn..." Amelia said with sympathy in her voice.

"I know, I know, it's far-fetched," he said, frustrated. Let's keep looking into Arron Reinhardt. It might be worth doing a social media search to see if we can find out more."

"Way ahead of you," Amelia said. She looked at her phone intently. Finn couldn't help but look her almost as intently. What were these feelings? It would have been so much simpler for him if he didn't have them. If he could have simply reconciled with Demi and got back to his old life. But the pull inside of him was not to something that already failed in the past, but instead to something positive in the future.

"Look at this," Amelia's finger tapped the screen sharply as she traced a hyperlink to its destination.

Finn leaned over, his eyes narrowing as they focused on the social media profile that materialized. "Arron Reinhardt's profile," he murmured.

"Yeah." She navigated deftly through the maze of posts and updates. "And here—" Her voice hitched slightly with anticipation as an image loaded, showing a small aircraft and a nondescript airstrip.

"Is that...?" Finn started.

"Gunner Airstrip," Amelia confirmed, tapping the caption beneath the photo. "Posted an hour ago. Says he's catching a plane home. Looks like it's a private flight. Gunner Airstrip is pretty small."

"Home..." Finn echoed, his thoughts racing. "How far?"

"Very close to Greenbridge."

"We need to get going, then."

"Turn around," Amelia's tone was brisk, leaving no room for argument. Finn complied, feeling the room shift as she moved behind him. The soft rustle of fabric suggested she was changing out of the robe, and he fought the curiosity edging into his consciousness.

"Peeking would be ungentlemanly," he remarked, attempting to dispel the tension with humor.

"Peeping would get you arrested," she shot back, the sound of a zipper punctuating her words.

"Maybe it'd be worth it." He grinned despite himself, hearing her scoff in response.

"Done. Let's go!"

"I need to grab my coat from my room!" Finn said loudly. "Then..."

Amelia grabbed her jacket, shrugging it on with swift movements. "Then, we've got a plane to stop."

CHAPTER NINETEEN

The moon hung low, a spectral observer in the ink-black sky, casting the junkyard in a pallid light that gave the scattered debris an otherworldly glow. The killer's footsteps crunched on gravel as he navigated through the labyrinth of automotive carcasses, each one a testament to stories ended untimely, much like the tales he himself concluded with cold finality.

"Yellow car, tires stacked... amateur theatrics," he muttered to himself, his voice barely audible above the whispering wind that danced through the skeletons of metal and rubber. His eyes, ever perceptive, scanned the chaotic tableau for the signal—a beacon amid the wreckage.

"Ah, there you are," he whispered as the old yellow car materialized from the shadows, its paint dulled by time, sitting solemnly with two tires perched atop its roof like a grotesque crown. He approached it with measured steps, the crunch of gravel underfoot syncing with the steady drumming of anticipation in his veins.

"Right where you said it'd be," he spoke into the void, acknowledging the absent partner in crime without warmth or gratitude. His hand reached out, the fingers finding the handle encrusted with grit and years of neglect, pulling open the creaking door of the vehicle.

"Stinks of modern decay," he noted, wrinkling his nose as the musty odor of mildew and rust assaulted his senses. How he wished to be flung back to a time of horses and knights.

The interior was coated with a fine layer of dust, undisturbed save for this single purpose. With practiced ease, he leaned across the threadbare seats toward the glove box, its latch giving way with an almost imperceptible click.

"Crude, but effective," he cooed as the compartment opened to reveal the handgun, nestled within as if it were resting in a cradle. His fingers caressed the cool metal with a lover's touch, extracting the weapon with reverence born not of respect but of utility. It was a tool, nothing more, yet in his hands, it promised to be the architect of fate. His only regret was that the weapon was more effective than an elegant dagger or bow.

"I'm glad he left you here for me. You will help me do something special, won't you? You'll punish those who value the modern world over the past, will you not?" he asked the gun, the barrel catching the moon's light as he inspected it. The magazine was full, the chamber eager. A small smile played upon his lips, a secret shared between artisan and instrument.

"Let slip the dogs of war!" he vowed, the promise hanging in the air like the flight of a medieval arrow. He closed the glove box with a soft thud, the sound swallowed whole by the sprawling graveyard of machinery around him.

If it were up to him, he'd put all of the modern world in its own grave, damned by its love for technology.

His mind wandered briefly to Finn, the image of his adversary conjured with a blend of contempt and anticipation. "You think you can anticipate my moves, don't you, Mr Wright? But you're playing checkers while I'm playing the ancient and superior game of chess."

The crisp bite of the night air filled his lungs as he emerged from the decrepit vehicle, a predator stepping out of a tomb of rust and abandonment. The gun slipped into his inside pocket with an ease that suggested long-held familiarity, its contours pressing against him like a secret talisman.

"Safe and sound, right where you belong," he muttered to the gun, his breath making transient clouds in the cold.

Around him, the junkyard lay silent, save for the occasional groan of metal, as if the derelict cars were stirring in their sleep. He cast a last lingering glance over his shoulder, ensuring no prying eyes had witnessed the transaction. Satisfied, he strode back to his own car, a nondescript model chosen for its ability to blend into any street, any scene.

"A steady hand is all that's required," he whispered to himself. His hand found the key in his pocket, the metal cool and solid—a promise of ignition, of motion.

He opened the driver's side door, the creaking hinge breaking the silence like a clandestine signal. Sliding behind the wheel, he sat in the momentary calm of the car's interior, where plans could be laid and futures woven from the threads of past grievances.

He thought of old generals and kings in centuries gone past, plotting their masterworks from their castles. This was an image he aspired to make his own.

"Patience," he counseled himself, the leather steering wheel familiar under his touch. "Every masterpiece takes time." He pictured Finn's face, etched with determination and unsuspecting of the blow that would soon fall. "You're just like the rest, valuing people like the Richmonds over heritage and history. Well, no more! You're going to wish you never crossed paths with me."

With a turn of the key, the engine roared to life, shattering the stillness and setting the stage for what was to come. The headlights cut through the dark, twin beacons heralding an unseen menace on the move.

"Tick tock, Finn," he said, the car's vibrations a harbinger of chaos. "The clock's winding down." His foot pressed down on the accelerator, the vehicle responding eagerly as it rolled forward, a shadow slipping away into the obscurity of the night.

As the junkyard receded into the distance, the killer felt the weight of the gun against his chest—an anchor to the reality of his mission. With each passing mile, the anticipation built, a crescendo of intent that promised to spill forth in a symphony of violence and retribution.

"Kings used to rule with an iron fist and show no mercy. Now, it's time for a history lesson," he intoned, the road ahead disappearing beneath the wheels, every turn taking him closer to destiny, to the next piece of his meticulously crafted vendetta.

CHAPTER TWENTY

The night was a tapestry of shadows and fleeting lights as Amelia's hands danced on the wheel, guiding the car through a labyrinth of country roads with the kind of precision that betrayed her police training. Finn's gaze was fixed on the dark horizon, but his mind was elsewhere, tethered to the phone pressed against his ear.

"Evening, this is Finn Wright," he said, voice steady despite the urgency pumping through his veins. "I need information on a flight leaving tonight."

"Ah, yes, Mr. Wright," crackled the voice of the airstrip manager on the other end. "We have one scheduled departure. It's just lining up now, actually."

Finn felt the grip of frustration, but he masked it with professional coolness. "Listen to me carefully," he instructed, words clipped. "That aircraft cannot leave the ground. I am working with Hertfordshire police on an urgent case."

Amelia shot him a look, one eyebrow arching in silent question, but she kept her focus on the road, swerving to avoid a pothole that emerged from the black like a hidden threat. The car's headlights cut through the darkness, a beacon in their high-stakes race against time.

"Are you sure about this?" the manager's voice wavered, the weight of responsibility suddenly anchoring his tone in seriousness. "We're nearly at takeoff."

"Absolutely sure," Finn affirmed, his past as a Special Agent lending authority to his command. "It's imperative you hold that plane. Lives could be at stake."

"I'll see what I can do, Mr. Wright." The manager's response was terse, signaling compliance.

"Hello?" Finn listened. The line had gone dead.

He tried to call again, but all he got was a busy signal.

Amelia gunned the engine, a silent symphony of gears and determination, while Finn disconnected the call. His fingers tapped a staccato rhythm on his knee, the only outward sign of the adrenaline coursing through him.

"Will they stop it?" Amelia's voice was calm, but Finn could hear the undercurrent of tension resonating with his own.

"They will," he stated, though his confidence was more a cloak for concern than a reflection of certainty. In the tight confines of the speeding vehicle, with every turn and twist of the road, Finn felt the chase tightening, a noose around the neck of the night. They were so close now, yet the specter of failure lurked, ready to snatch victory from their grasp at the last second.

"Good," she replied, eyes fixed on the tarmac ahead, her resolve as unshakable as the ground beneath them. "Because we're almost there, and I don't fancy a wild goose chase across Europe."

"Neither do I," Finn muttered, scanning the horizon for any sign of their quarry. He adjusted his grip on the phone, prepared to make another call if necessary. But deep down, he hoped it wouldn't come to that, hoped that the next turn in the road would bring them within reach of justice.

Finn's doubts got the better of him. He called again, and this time the number rang, with the same answer.

"This is Finn Wright again," he said, trying not to sound annoyed. "We got cut off. I just wanted to make sure we were on the same page. Have you grounded the plane yet?"

"I've had a talk with the airstrip owner, and..."

"Listen, you must hold that plane!" Finn's voice was firm, a steel edge hidden beneath the soft lamplight spilling into the car from the overhead streetlights.

"Sir, I—I'm not sure I can—" The manager's voice crackled through the phone speaker, a mixture of bewilderment and rising panic.

"Think about it. If you let that jet take off, you're aiding a fugitive. Hertfordshire police authority is behind this request," Finn interjected, cutting through the manager's hesitation like a scalpel. "We're a minute away, and if that plane hasn't been ordered to switch off its engines, you'll be escorted off that airstrip and straight to a cell!"

A pause hung in the air, heavy with unspoken consequences, until the manager capitulated with an audible gulp. "Right. I'll do it. I'm heading to the control tower now."

"Make it fast," Finn urged, before ending the call.

The night rushed by as Amelia took another sharp turn, the tires protesting against the asphalt. Ahead, the airstrip unfolded like a dormant beast, the runway lights flickering like sleepy eyes about to be rudely awakened.

"There," Finn pointed, his keen eyes latching onto the silhouette of a small passenger jet at the far end of the tarmac. It was poised for departure, its engines humming a low, ominous tune that spoke of imminent escape.

"Doesn't look like it's stopping," he murmured more to himself than to Amelia, his mind racing through their options. "God damned liars!"

"Then we'd better make sure it does," Amelia replied, determination lacing her words as she pressed harder on the accelerator, the car responding with a surge of power.

Finn's gaze never left the jet, watching for any sign of compliance, any indication that the manager had been true to his word. But as they drew nearer, the plane began to inch forward, its pace gradually quickening.

"Damn it," Finn cursed under his breath. He could almost see the pilot inside, oblivious or indifferent to the storm they were bringing down upon him. Finn reached for his seat belt, clicking it into place with a decisive snap. His mind was already leaping ahead, calculating the narrow window of opportunity they had left.

"It's too dangerous to chase the jet, we need to ground it from the control tower," Amelia stated, though it was less of an observation and more of a directive.

"I can keep it down, Amelia!," Finn said, frustration etched into his face.

"It's too risky, to you and the passengers."

As the car ate up the distance between them and the control tower, Finn felt the familiar thrill of the chase sharpen his focus. Every second mattered now, every decision could tip the scales. They were in the dance of predator and prey, the outcome hanging by a thread as thin and taut as the night air itself.

The control tower loomed against the backdrop of the starless sky, a solitary beacon in the dark. Amelia's foot eased off the accelerator as they approached, gravel crunching under tires announcing their arrival. She parked with precision, a swift motion that betrayed her urgency without descending into recklessness.

"Stay here," she commanded, her tone leaving no room for debate as she threw open the door and stepped out into the cool night air.

Finn watched her silhouette merge with the shadows, the determined set of her shoulders speaking volumes. The manager, a middle-aged man with spectacles perched precariously on his nose, emerged from the tower like a startled owl roused from its perch. He was waving his hands, the universal sign of distress.

"Keep that plane on the ground!" Amelia shouted.

"I can't!" the manager called out, voice cracking. "The captain—no response to any hails. It's like he's vanished into thin air!"

"Or following orders... Damn it," Finn muttered under his breath. His keen mind raced, piecing together the fragments of an increasingly complex puzzle. He could almost see the invisible threads of the investigation spinning out, weaving a web that ensnared them all.

"Keep trying," Amelia shot back, authority crackling in her voice. "We need that plane grounded yesterday."

As Amelia engaged the manager, Finn's gaze darted to the airstrip where the jet's engines hummed with a low, ominous threat. Time was slipping through their fingers. He cast a glance at Amelia, then made a split-second decision; the kind that had defined his career and too often, his life.

"Sorry, Winters," he shouted, already vaulting over the center console into the driver's seat. "I think you'll get into trouble if you come with me."

"Wait, what—Finn, no!" Amelia's protest sliced through the night, sharp as the wind that tugged at his jacket when he slammed the door shut.

The car roared to life beneath him, the familiar vibration a comforting ally as he shifted gears. He spared a final glance at Amelia, her figure framed by the stark floodlights of the tower, before he floored the accelerator.

Finn's thoughts careened with the speedometer's needle: plans, contingencies, the myriad ways this could unfold. Each scenario played out in his head, a chess game where he needed to think ten moves ahead. There was no turning back now. He was committed to the path, to the chase, to the justice that awaited at the end of this runway.

And somewhere in the symphony of screeching tires and racing engines, Finn found a grim sort of solace. This was his element, the chaos where clarity was born, where he could strip away the noise and hear the truth whispering amid the tumult.

"Come on, Reinhardt," he murmured to the darkness. "If you're innocent, why leave?"

The runway stretched before Finn like a challenge, the asphalt a tarmac titan daring him to take it on. The plane was already taxiing, its silhouette a darker smudge against the night sky. Finn's hands clenched the wheel tighter, every muscle coiled as he urged the car forward.

"Keep going," he whispered, feeling the rumble of the engine through the soles of his feet. The world outside blurred into streaks of light and shadow as he pushed the vehicle faster, the chase thrumming in his blood.

"Reinhardt!" he spat out the name like a curse, his jaw set. He could see the small passenger jet gaining speed, its engines howling their impatience to be airborne.

"This might be the dumbest thing I've ever done," he muttered. "But you are not getting away, now, are you?" he said half to himself, half to the fleeing figure he knew sat within that metal bird. The question hung in the air, unanswered, save for the roar of engines—both his and the plane's.

"Time to clip your wings," Finn decided, the car now close enough to the moving plane that he could almost touch it. His focus narrowed, the rest of the world fading until there was only this moment, this heartbeat of action.

He drew up alongside the rear of the aircraft, his gaze flickering between the runway and the target. Then, with a calculated precision born of years in the field, he angled the car just so—metal kissed metal with a screech that clawed at the night.

"Gotcha," Finn exhaled as he felt the impact judder through the frame of the car, the plane's tail nudging under the force.

For an endless second, everything seemed suspended—the chase, the night, even his breath. And then, as though conceding defeat, the plane slowed, inch by reluctant inch, until it rolled to a complete stop.

"I can't actually believe that worked," Finn said, though the words were lost in the cacophony of victory and spinning wheels. He allowed himself a tight smile, knowing the game had changed. This was no longer about chase; it was about confrontation.

Finn's boots hit the tarmac with a determined thud, the echoes of his car door slamming shut swallowed by the vastness of the night. The airstrip was a ribbon of dimly lit asphalt, the control tower lights cast long shadows that danced to the rhythm of his pounding footsteps. He didn't wait for his heart rate to settle; there wasn't time.

A sprinter's energy surged in his legs, propelling him towards the small passenger jet, its engines winding down with a groan of thwarted escape. He searched with his grip and found a part of the plane on which to pull himself up. Once he had footing above the ground, his hand found the cold metal of the plane's door, rapping sharply against it—a staccato burst echoing the urgency coursing through his veins.

"Open up!" he barked, his voice slicing through the residual hum of the engine.

There was a moment's hesitation, a brief standoff between silence and action, before the latch clinked, and the door swung outward. A blast of cabin air rushed past Finn, tinged with the scent of apprehension and expensive cologne.

"Hello there," Finn said, head thrust into the artificial calm of the cabin, eyes locking onto the figure strapped into one of the plush seats. The man's face was a landscape of worry, creased with the anticipation of a confrontation he no doubt wished to avoid.

"Going somewhere, Mr. Reinhardt? And without saying bye, too." Finn's words were edged with a grin, not out of amusement but as a display of power—the cat that cornered the mouse reveling in the final play.

CHAPTER TWENTY ONE

Finn knew he was exhausted, still in a weakened state, but his mind was alive with the thought that he had the killer, and potentially one of Vilne's associates, in his grasp at last.

The fluorescent lights in the interview room at the Hertfordshire constabulary buzzed with a muted persistence, casting a clinical pallor over the scene. Finn sat with an unfaltering gaze fixed on Arron Reinhardt. The man was the picture of composed wealth in his tailored suit, his posture relaxed in a manner that seemed studied and deliberate. Across the table, Amelia Winters mirrored Finn's intensity, her sharp eyes never wavering from the suspect.

"Mr. Reinhardt," Finn finally broke the silence, his voice steady and low, "you seem awfully comfortable for a man in your position."

Arron's lips twitched into a half-smile, his fingers interlaced on the table in front of him. "Well, Agent Wright, comfort is a state of mind, isn't it?" he replied smoothly.

"Is it now?" Amelia chimed in, her tone cool but edged with steel. "I'd imagine comfort is hard to come by under scrutiny for serious crimes."

Finn leaned back in his chair, his mind racing through the implications of Arron's nonchalance. Was it innocence or arrogance that kept the man so unnervingly calm? He glanced briefly at the recorder, its red light a silent sentinel, capturing every nuance of the conversation.

"Look," Arron said, his annoyance beginning to crack his polished veneer, "if you're not going to ask me any questions, may I be excused? Time is money, after all."

"Money..." Finn mused aloud, letting the word hang in the air as he locked eyes with Arron once again. "That seems to be a recurring theme with you, Mr. Reinhardt."

Amelia leaned forward, resting her arms on the table. "We have plenty of questions, Mr. Reinhardt," she assured him. "Just taking our time to ask the right ones."

"Time that I'm sure your expensive lawyer is billing you for by the minute," Finn added, a slight smirk playing at the corner of his mouth.

"Indeed, they are," Arron conceded, his mask of composure slipping further. "So why don't we expedite this process, because as soon as my lawyer is here, you'll be the one in trouble."

"Expedite..." Finn echoed thoughtfully, the gears turning in his head. He was aware of the delicate dance of interrogation, each step measured and precise. He knew the value of patience, of letting the silence do the heavy lifting. But more than that, he understood the power of the unspoken – the threat of what remained unsaid.

"Patience, Mr. Reinhardt," Amelia said, her voice a calm counterpart to Finn's tacit tension. "All in due time. I think your legal representation is heading from London, so we just need to wait, unless you feel confident enough to proceed on your own."

Finn loved that approach. It was a challenge to a man who clearly had a rather unhinged ego.

"Fine," Arron huffed, shifting in his seat, the first clear sign of discomfort since he had walked into the room. "But let's get on with it, shall we?"

"Let's," Finn agreed, his eyes never leaving the suspect's face. In that moment, he felt the familiar surge of adrenaline, the quiet thrill of the chase. It was a feeling he had known many times before, a sensation that reminded him why he did this work, despite everything it had cost him. And as the tape continued to run, recording every syllable and sigh, Finn knew that the game was afoot, and he was exactly where he needed to be.

"Recognize this, do you?" Finn's voice was clipped as he slid a series of glossy photographs across the smooth surface of the interview table. They landed in front of Arron Reinhardt with the precision of dealt cards. The images were stark, revealing the plush interior of a private jet, all cream leather and polished wood.

"Of course," Arron replied, his tone dry, barely glancing at the first photo before flicking it aside with a manicured finger. "It's hard to forget a G650 when you've spent the better part of six hours in one."

"Indeed," Finn murmured, pressing on. "Then perhaps you'll find it peculiar that your pilot seemed to have an aversion to communicating with the control tower during your little jaunt."

"Shouldn't you be asking him that?" Arron retorted smoothly, though Finn caught the briefest flicker of annoyance in his gaze.

Before Arron could further deflect, Amelia leaned forward, her movement deliberate, introducing a new photograph into the interrogation's delicate ballet. This one showed the cargo hold, utilitarian and cold, a stark contrast to the luxury of the cabin.

"Does this look familiar too?" she asked, her eyes sharp as flint, watching for any telltale fracture in Arron's facade

He took a longer look this time, his fingers pausing mid-twitch. "It's a cargo hold," he said finally, a touch of disdain creeping into his voice. "They're all quite similar."

Finn noted the slight tightening around Arron's eyes, the way his fingers betrayed a tremor as they rested on the table. He sensed the shift in the room's atmosphere, like the charged silence before lightning strikes. Every detail was a puzzle piece, and Finn knew that patience was necessary to place them correctly.

"Similar, maybe," Finn agreed, but his thoughts weaved through the facts they already knew, connecting dots that Arron hoped would remain disparate. "But not many have the exact configuration we found on this particular flight. It's... unique."

Arron's response was a calculated shrug, but Finn wasn't swayed by the veneer of indifference. He could almost hear the cogs turning in Arron's head, the same way they churned in his own. The game of cat-and-mouse continued, both men aware that every second ticking by was another moment closer to truth or consequence.

"Unique or not," Arron said, recovering some of his earlier confidence, "I'm just a passenger. I don't poke around in cargo holds."

"Of course not," Amelia chimed in, her skepticism clear as she folded her arms. "That'd be beneath someone of your stature."

"Quite right," Arron smirked, but there was an edge to it now, the faintest hint of steel beneath the silk of his words.

Finn leaned back, letting the silence stretch between them again, a taut line ready to snap. In his mind, scenarios played out like scenes from films he'd seen, each possibility a route to explore, a potential trap to set. The photographs were just the beginning, a prelude to the crescendo he felt building in the depths of the case. As Arron met his stare with cool defiance, Finn knew the dance was far from over – but he intended to lead.

The air in the interview room felt heavier as Finn flicked another photograph across the table. It landed with a soft slap, its glossy surface reflecting the harsh overhead lights. The image, an unassuming cargo hold, seemed innocuous enough until Amelia's finger tapped insistently on a panel that didn't quite align with the aircraft's inner wall.

"Found this little number tucked away behind here," she said, her voice betraying no emotion, yet somehow it hung in the air like a threat.

Arron's eyes darted to the image, then away, a bead of sweat tracing a path down his temple despite the coolness of the room. His fingers gripped the armrests of his chair, knuckles whitening against the dark leather. "A hidden compartment?" he echoed, attempting nonchalance but only managing to strain his voice slightly. "Sounds like a mystery novel."

"Reality often outdoes fiction, Mr. Reinhardt," Finn interjected. "Especially when it comes to illegal goods, historic items and antiques—quite the collection you've amassed. And with flight records going all around the world, I wonder if you have a business for dealing in priceless antiques... Stolen ones."

"I assure you, I know nothing about this." Arron's attempt at recovery was swift, but the slight tremor in his voice betrayed his composure. "I merely take flights, not inventory."

"You take more than that," Finn retorted. "Looking at your movements, the way you conduct yourself, the fact that the pilot wasn't even willing to listen to the control tower, it all boils down to crime. You are *very* successful. From the information we've received in the last hour, you have been investigated before by the FBI, no less, but somehow slithered your way out of facing up to your own crimes. Not today. Your operation stops here. There are two murdered people from the States, and they are pointing straight to you as their killer. That flight is the last one you'll take as a free man for some time. Ironic that the flight itself is what has incriminated you."

"Sounds like complete fiction! Like I said," he reiterated, a vein bulging now on his forehead. "I was just a passenger."

"Yet, the manifest," Amelia leaned forward, placing the document before him with precision, "suggests otherwise. It seems 'just a passenger' doesn't quite capture your involvement."

"Manifests can be misleading." Arron's retort came too quickly, his eyes now scanning the room as if seeking an escape route from the truth.

"Or illuminating," Finn countered smoothly. "They shine a light on details, like who charters planes. And according to this," he tapped the paper pointedly, "that person is you."

"Paperwork. Bureaucracy." Arron's laugh was devoid of humor, a hollow sound that bounced off the sterile walls. "It's all semantics."

"Semantics that place you at the center of a smuggling operation," Amelia stated, her gaze unwavering.

Finn watched Arron closely, reading the minute shifts in his posture, the way his eyes refused to settle. The suspect was unraveling, thread by precarious thread, and with each word, each piece of evidence laid bare, they were one step closer to snaring him in the web of his own deceit. The room was silent for a moment, save for the faint hum of the recording device, capturing every nuance of their exchange.

"Being a passenger on your own chartered plane filled with contraband doesn't look good for you," Finn said quietly, allowing the implication to hang between them, a specter of guilt that couldn't be easily dispelled.

"Looks can be deceiving," Arron managed, but his glance toward the door spoke volumes.

"Indeed, they can," Finn agreed, his mind already racing ahead to the next move in this high-stakes game.

Finn leaned back in his chair, the metal frame groaning under the subtle shift of weight. He slid a set of black-and-white photographs across the nondescript gray table, their edges skating over the surface with a hushed whisper. The images, stark depictions of ornate relics and intricate tapestries, settled into Arron Reinhardt's line of sight.

"Recognize any of these?" Finn's voice was level, his eyes locked on Arron, searching for the telltale flutter of guilt. "They have quite the history, you know, and I wonder if some will be traced back to Richmond Castle."

Arron's fingers twitched, betraying him as they reached out before curling back. His facade cracked, lines of strain etching themselves deeper around his eyes. "Richmond Castle? I have nothing to do with that place."

Finn's gaze didn't waver. "But you've been rather vocal about the renovations there, haven't you? Quite the local activist." He paused, allowing the statement to settle. "Or is it more accurate to say you saw an opportunity among the controversy?"

"Activism isn't a crime," Arron retorted, but the nervous energy radiating from him filled the cramped interview room like a pungent perfume.

"Perhaps not," Amelia chimed in, her tone sharp as broken glass. "But smuggling artifacts is."

"Smuggling?" Arron's laugh was meant to be dismissive, but it came out strained, like the last gasps of air from a deflating balloon.

"Indeed," Finn confirmed with a nod. "And at the very least, Mr. Reinhardt, we're charging you with that crime. Smuggling artifacts from what appears to be a number of national treasures. And we're keeping you here for further questioning regarding the murders of Lily and Thomas Richmond."

"Murders?" Arron's composure crumbled, his voice cracking under the weight of implication. "You think I had something to do with that? There's nothing on that plane from them."

"Let's just say you're a person of interest." Finn's words were cold, precise.

"It might be true," Amelia added. "That you didn't take anything from Richmond Castle, but we believe you scouted the place out with the intention to steal something valuable. Then, something went wrong, you were rumbled by the Richmonds, and you resorted to murder."

"I didn't do it," the man replied, firmly.

"If we are to believe you," Finn offered, "Then, you might have something of interest to us that could help show your innocence. We believe your phone might hold some valuable information. Someone took photos of Richmond Castle before the murders, and I wonder if they can be found on your phone."

"I want my lawyer," Arron demanded, his hands forming into fists that betrayed his attempt at remaining calm.

"Of course, you're entitled to one," Amelia replied smoothly, though her hand hovered near the recorder, ready to halt its operation at a moment's notice.

"Your phone, Mr. Reinhardt," Finn reiterated, extending his hand across the table with an unspoken ultimatum.

"No," Arron snapped, pulling back. "You have no right—"

"Actually, we do," Finn cut in, his tone brokering no argument. "We can take it as evidence and get a court order to unlock it. Or you could make this easier on yourself. Either way, we're getting your phone. If you help, it could look good for you, they might go a little easier on you for the smuggling, if you help us catch a murderer."

The silence stretched taut between them, a high wire upon which Arron's fate teetered precariously.

"Fine," he spat out finally, his fingers trembling as he retrieved the sleek device from his jacket pocket. "The code is 3529."

"Thank you," Finn said, pocketing the phone as if it were an ordinary exchange. "We'll be sure everything is done by the book."

With a nod to Amelia, Finn stood up, his movements deliberate, the latent power of his former Special Agent training evident in every step. Together, they exited the room, leaving Arron alone with the echo of the door closing behind them—a sound that, to Arron Reinhardt, must have seemed very much like the sealing of a tomb.

Outside the sterile walls of the interview room, the precinct was a hive of activity, uniformed officers and detectives scurrying to their duties with the urgency of a clock's second hand. Finn and Amelia found refuge in a narrow corridor lined with bulletin boards plastered with case notes and faded photographs of people whose fates were frozen in time.

"Reinhardt's sweating," Finn began, his voice low as he scanned the corridor for eavesdroppers. "And it's not because of the room's temperature."

Amelia leaned against the cool concrete wall, arms folded. "Agreed. He's too polished to let nerves show without good reason." She tilted her head slightly, her eyes narrowing. "The cargo hold photo hit a nerve. If we match any of those antiques to Richmond Castle..."

"Then he's our man," Finn concluded, tapping his fingers against his thigh in thought. "Reinhardt knew about the renovations, had access, motive, and now means."

"Means?" Amelia prompted, her brow raised in question.

"An antique dirk." Finn's gaze met hers, steady and certain. "A weapon fit for a crime of passion—or profit."

"Assuming it was among the smuggled goods." She unfolded her arms, reaching into her pocket for her phone to check the latest updates from forensics. "We were told nothing was missing from the castle, but it's such a large place. Parker, the caretaker, might just not have noticed yet."

"Right on." Finn sighed, scratching the stubble along his jaw. The weight of past cases seemed to press upon his shoulders, his mind relentlessly sifting through details, searching for connections. "Or the Richmond's had it hidden for their own reasons."

"I wonder if the Richmonds themselves were involved in smuggling," Amelia said. "Just a thought, considering Thomas Richmond's cargo business."

"I don't know about that. I'll admit, I thought Max Vilne was behind this for that reason, that he could have been smuggled into the UK using Thomas Richmond's business practices. His signature is all over the chaos," Finn confessed, reluctant yet honest. "But nothing links him directly to the Richmonds' deaths."

"Perhaps Reinhardt's our missing link to Vilne," Amelia suggested, though her tone held more hope than conviction.

"Maybe." Finn wasn't ready to discard any thread that might unravel the truth. "We should look through the phone for any clues. But... Could you give me a moment? I have something on my mind and I need to make a call."

"Demi?" Amelia guessed, her sharp intuition cutting straight to the matter.

"Yeah," he said, the word tasting bitter on his tongue. Demi's shadow loomed large in his life, a constant reminder of vulnerabilities he could ill afford. "Just for a moment. I felt I was a bit sharp with her earlier. If you don't mind, then I'll look at this phone."

"Okay," she said. "But remember, people besides Demi are counting on us. The Richmond's family for one."

Finn nodded, the air of the station suddenly stifling as he pushed through the double doors and out into the brisk evening. The sky above Garden City was streaked with clouds and stars, an oil painting punctuated by the silhouettes of buildings. He dialed Demi's number, each ring gnawing at his resolve until her voice came through, laced with that familiar tension.

"Hey, it's me," Finn said, his words steady despite the turmoil beneath. "Just checking in. Are you safe?"

"Hi, you've reached Demi, sorry you can't reach me..."

Finn hung up the answering message. He looked up at the stars and breathed in the cold air. Then, he turned and went back inside. But Demi was still sharp in his mind, and her safety would not leave his thoughts.

CHAPTER TWENTY TWO

The corridor outside the interview room was a sterile expanse of linoleum and fluorescent light. Finn leaned against the cool wall, his gaze lingering on the closed door as he fished out his cellphone with a practiced hand. With a thumb that remembered every contour of her number, he dialed Demi again, listening to the trill of the ringtone that seemed too cheerful for the tense silence that surrounded him.

"Come on, Demi," he muttered under his breath. The phone continued its electronic serenade to no avail. Voicemail greeted him, once more, impersonal and brisk. Finn's jaw tightened, and he ended the call without leaving a message. He couldn't shake the feeling that she was avoiding his calls on purpose.

With a sigh, Finn's attention shifted to the object of interest in his other hand—Arron Reinhardt's confiscated phone. His fingers danced over the screen, entering the security pin code with the ease of someone who had done this more times than he cared to count. The familiar click sound confirmed his entry, and the phone's contents spilled open in front of him like a digital Pandora's box.

"Let's see what secrets you're holding," Finn murmured, swiping through the interface. Apps and folders flickered past, each an unspoken chapter of Arron's life.

Finn's thumb hovered over the messaging icon on Arron Reinhardt's phone, his anticipation a silent hum in his veins. A tap, and the screen shifted to reveal an empty void where one would expect a clutter of communications—an expanse of digital nothingness.

"Clean as a whistle," Finn muttered under his breath, eyes narrowing. "Too clean."

He rubbed at the stubble on his chin, the slight abrasion grounding him in thought. Could IT work their magic on this? he wondered but knew better than to hope blindly. The department's tech wizards had a knack for resurrecting lost data, yet some ghosts were determined to stay buried.

"Messages deleted," he spoke into the air, almost expecting the walls to hold counsel with him. "But why scrub it so thoroughly, Reinhardt? What are you so desperate to hide?"

His finger swiped through the phone's gallery next, the flicker of images casting shadows across his focused expression. He paused on photographs of stately homes, their regal facades marred by poor composition and erratic focus.

"Blown highlights and cut-off spires," Finn scrutinized aloud, his voice tinged with professional disdain. "You never had much respect for the craft, did you, Arron?"

He felt the pieces of the puzzle jostling for position in his mind, each photo a clue in the grander scheme. His gaze fell upon a picture of a grandiose manor, its stone lions standing sentinel at the gates.

"Chillingham Castle, or is it...?" Finn trailed off, realization dawning. He looked at the tagged data. "No, it's Highclere—my word, they're all here. From North to South."

The energy in the hallway shifted, charged with the acute awareness that each image was a breadcrumb leading to a truth yet unveiled. Finn's thumb swiped with precision, cataloging the visual inventory of England's aristocratic heritage as seen through the lens of a criminal mind.

"From Cornwall to Cumbria," he continued, the rhythm of his words a metronome to his racing thoughts. "What were you after, Reinhardt? Not just souvenirs, I reckon."

The action of scrolling became mechanical, the estate after estate parading before his eyes, yet Finn's thoughts were far from the device in his hand. They took flight, soaring over the rolling hills and manicured gardens, seeking the connection between the images and the crime.

"Stately homes," Finn broke the silence again, addressing the empty space before him as if it held the key. "And what lies within."

The notion settled heavily within him, a weighty conviction that he was peering through a window into Arron Reinhardt's clandestine excursions—a voyeur to the prelude of something sinister.

"IT might not get back the texts," Finn acknowledged, pocketing the phone with a decisive click. "But these photos...they speak volumes."

With a deep breath, Finn prepared to step back into the fray, the images imprinted in his memory. Each pixelated facade was now etched with urgency, a silent siren call to action. It was time to bring the unspoken narrative of those pictures to light, to expose the darkness lurking behind the splendor of historic stone and mortar.

But something then bothered him. Something that his brain had picked up but had yet to fully reveal to him.

Finn tapped the screen of Arron's phone, his fingers deftly navigating through the labyrinth of apps and icons again. The dull hum of the precinct buzzed around him, each officer orbiting their own centers of gravity, their own cases. But within Finn's grasp, he held a sliver of another world—a digital trove that beckoned with silent promises of revelation.

"Ah," Finn murmured as an icon flickered under his touch, revealing a second online gallery that hadn't been apparent before. His thumb hovered over it. "What have you got hidden away here, Reinhardt?"

With a tap, the screen filled with thumbnails, a mosaic of antiquities and grandeur. Finn scrolled, eyes flickering as he absorbed the images: a mahogany grandfather clock, its intricate carvings a testament to a craftsman's pride; a porcelain vase, blue patterns dancing across its curved belly; a tapestry, woven with the vibrant threads of history.

"Look at this," Finn said softly, almost to himself. He took in the grandiosity captured in the photos—the sprawling lawns, the imposing facades. These were places steeped in time, each frame a window into England's storied past.

He switched back to the images stored on the phone, noticing the abrupt shift in quality. Reinhardt's attempts at photography were akin to a child's crude finger paintings compared to the masterful strokes on an artist's canvas. Fingers clumsy, focus askew, the images were devoid of the finesse that marked the online collection.

"Amateur hour, isn't it?" Finn chuckled dryly, the sound hollow in the relative quiet.

Switching once more, he scrutinized the online images. "Someone knows their way around a camera. And these places..." His voice trailed off as he zoomed in on a photo, tracing the lines of a stately home's architecture with his eyes. "Not just snapshots. Studies."

"Reinhardt's work is...lacking." Finn's gaze was unyielding as it darted between the two sets of images. "But this other person—there's intent behind the lens. Skill apparent in every shot."

The wheels in his mind churned, piecing together fragments of a puzzle that grew more complex with each swipe. The disparity was too stark, the skill gap too wide. There was another player in this game— one who saw through a different lens, quite literally.

"Who are you?" Finn whispered, trailing a finger along the edge of the phone. The question lingered in the air, unanswered but heavy with implication. Whoever this photographer was, they held the key to unraveling the mystery that had entangled itself around the grandeur of England's heritage sites.

Finn hunched over the phone, his fingers navigating through the pictures again, wanting to be sure. The sleek device felt incongruous in his calloused hands, a reminder of the digital breadcrumbs that could either forge connections or sever them entirely. His eyes narrowed as he flicked back and forth between the amateurish shots stored locally and the polished images held in the cloud.

"Two photographers," he murmured to himself, "as different as chalk from cheese. Better run this past Amelia," Finn decided, pocketing the phone once again. "There's more to this than meets the eye—or Reinhardt's clumsy trigger finger."

With purpose in his stride, Finn headed towards the interview room, the images burned into his brain, the dichotomy between them fueling his determination. It was a silent symphony of clues, and Finn Wright was ready to conduct his search for the truth.

He pocketed Reinhardt's phone into his jacket pocket. The observation area outside the interview room was silent, save for the hum of fluorescent lights and the distant clatter of activity elsewhere in the station. Finn shook his head slightly, a silent rebuke of the shoddy workmanship in Arron's photographs. Whoever had shared those online images had an eye for detail that Arron sorely lacked.

Pushing open the door to the interview room, Finn caught Amelia's gaze; she was poised, her attention never straying from the man across the table. Arron Reinhardt looked like a bird caught in a snare, his posture rigid, eyes darting around the room—a stark contrast to Amelia's calm demeanor as she sat watching.

"Who took these photos, Arron?" Finn asked, his voice threading through the tension in the room.

Arron's Adam's apple bobbed as he struggled to form words, his lips parting and closing with no sound emerging.

"Because these," Finn continued, pulling out the phone and sliding it across the table towards Reinhardt, "are not the work of the same person who has access to this online collection."

His tone was light, almost teasing, but his eyes were sharp. "Come now, surely you must know your own limitations with a camera. These snaps are... well, let's just say they're not winning any awards."

Arron's hand trembled visibly as he picked up the phone, his gaze flitting between the two detectives. A bead of sweat traced a path down his temple.

"Someone else is quite the shutterbug, aren't they?" Finn leaned in, resting his forearms on the cold metal table. "A partner, perhaps?"

The silence stretched, filled only by the soft whir of the air conditioning unit. The question hung between them, laden with implications. Finn observed Arron closely, reading the man's every micro-expression.

"Who is it, Arron?" Amelia prompted gently yet firmly, tipping the scales.

Arron's mouth opened again, but this time a faint whisper escaped, "I—"

"Your artistic friend," Finn interjected smoothly, "they're really quite talented. It would be a shame if their real work went unrecognized and someone else was held responsible, would it not?"

Arron's eyes flickered, a flash of fear—or was it resignation?—passing over his features. Finn's pulse quickened as he sensed the breakthrough within reach, each second drawing out like the ticking of a clock counting down to revelation.

Arron Reinhardt sat, the muscles in his jaw clenched so tightly that they twitched. His hands lay flat on the table, fingers splayed as if trying to anchor himself against the tide of accusations.

"Arron," Amelia's voice sliced through the tension, her words deliberate and clear. "We're not here to play games. We know there's someone else involved." Finn loved how quickly Amelia caught on, often it was him playing catch up with her, but either way as detectives, they kept pace with each other.

"Even if I knew, why would I tell you?" Arron spat out, defiance laced with a hint of desperation.

"Because," Amelia leaned in closer, her gaze unwavering, "if you don't, we'll have no choice but to assume you're just as guilty of murder as you are of smuggling." She paused, letting the gravity of her statement sink into Arron's consciousness.

Finn noticed the subtle shift in Arron's posture, the way his shoulders hunched slightly inward. He was breaking.

"Look, Arron," Finn chimed in, his tone a mixture of empathy and authority, "this isn't about pinning everything on you. It's about finding the truth. Help us help you."

Arron's eyes darted between Finn and Amelia, seeking an escape that wasn't there. Finally, he let out a long, resigned sigh. "Fine," he muttered, his voice almost lost in the quiet of the room. "It's Sandler.

Steven Sandler. His details are in my phone."

"Is he particularly short?" Amelia asked without missing a beat, her intuition already piecing together the puzzle.

"Yeah, yeah he is," Arron confirmed, his defeat evident in his slumped posture.

Finn exchanged a look with Amelia, both their minds racing towards the same conclusion. The upward trajectory of Thomas Richmond's stab wounds had been puzzling them from the start, but now, with this new information, the pieces began to align. The killer wasn't a woman, but a man of shorter stature.

"Good," Amelia said, her voice softening just enough to acknowledge Arron's cooperation. "Thank you, Arron. You've just made things a lot clearer for us. You're still going down for smuggling."

"Is this guy into your smuggling ring?" Finn asked.

"He's an Historian, if you must ask," Arron said. "And a damned good one. He cares about history and makes a point of documenting it."

Finn laughed in disbelief. "So, let me get this straight, the guy isn't even a smuggler? You just have him taking pictures of places and artifacts around the UK, then, unbeknownst to him, you pick places you can plunder from his photos and info?"

Arron's color drained from his face. "I want my lawyer."

"Oh, Buddy!" Finn said, loudly. "You thought you were taking advantage of him, but it turns out the Historian is a violent killer who'll knock people off who are, in his mind, defacing tradition. And that's all led to your smuggling days being numbered. Unlucky. You should have taken all the photos yourself."

"I don't understand..." the man said in disbelief.

"The Historian went there to kill," Amelia put it more bluntly.

"But he wanted to keep on killing," Finn said. "So he didn't want to get caught. He scouted out the place as per your instructions when looking for artifacts you could steal and sell on the black market. You no doubt didn't want anyone dead, but he did. He had revenge on his mind, probably for all the renovations at the castle. It hurt how important he felt history was. But the man intended to make the kill look like an accident. Instead, Thomas Richmond entered the study at the castle suddenly, and the Historian resorted to brute force. That explains the mixed signals we were getting at the crime scene – half planned, half accidental. He killed using an old dirk that I suspect he found hidden in the study somewhere. Perhaps the very thing you wanted stolen?"

All Arron could do was shake his hands in disbelief.

"I still suspect that someone else has been prodding Steven Sandler," Finn said. "A man named Max Vilne. You better pray you don't have any connections to him, because when I'm done with Sandler, I'll find out."

Finn stood up, the chair scraping against the floor with a sharp sound that seemed to echo the urgency building inside him. It was time to act, and every second counted now. They were one step closer to putting an end to this once and for all.

"We should get moving," Finn said, his voice steady but laden with the weight of urgency as he strode towards the door. He reached for the handle, feeling the cool metal against his palm, an anchor in the storm of activity that was about to ensue.

"If you can keep up," Amelia replied, her fingers dancing across her phone's screen with practiced speed.

"Please tell me you aren't playing a game?" Finn asked.

"I'm sending a message to Rob and Inspector Wilson that they we made a breakthrough," she said. "Keep everyone in the loop."

"Now, we can go," she said with a seductive smile. The air between them crackled with the anticipation of the chase.

As they burst from the interview room, Finn's mind was a tumultuous sea of thoughts and deductions. Sandler, an historian with a grudge was masquerading as nothing more than a diminutive, harmless photographer, yet potentially harboring psychopathic tendencies. The image of the meticulous stab wounds, ascending like a sinister crescendo, played over in his mind—a morbid signature left by someone who could navigate the world largely unnoticed.

Finn looked at the phone as he ran. "Looks like the Steven Sandler contact has an address. Another damned hotel. If I see one more hotel today, I'm going to have to become a tour guide!"

"This is it, Finn," Amelia said as they headed out of the building, down the steps and towards their parked car.

He nodded once, not wasting any breath on promises or bravado. The door slammed shut with a resounding thud behind him, sealing him within the confines of his vehicle. As the engine roared to life beneath his touch, Finn allowed himself a single thought that wasn't centered on the task at hand—Demi. Wherever she was, he hoped she was safe. Shaking the distraction from his head, he shifted into gear and peeled out from the curb, the chase for Steven Sandler consuming his entire being.

CHAPTER TWENTY THREE

The police car's tires bit into the gravel with urgency, spitting up tiny stones as Finn Wright brought the vehicle to a halt outside the squat structure of the travel hotel. The place was nondescript, its brickwork tinged with years of neglect—a perfect hideout for someone who didn't want to be found. Finn's gaze swept over the parking lot, hunting for any sign of movement that might betray their quarry's presence.

"Here," Amelia said tersely, barely waiting for the car to stop before her hand was on the door handle. "This is it."

Finn nodded, his senses alert, as they both stepped out into the biting air. He followed Amelia, noting how her coat flapped against her in the wind, a silent testament to her determination. They crossed the threshold of the hotel lobby, a bell above the door jangling their arrival.

"Can I help you?" The receptionist, a young woman with an anxious expression, peered at them from behind her computer screen.

"Steven Sandler," Amelia stated, badge in hand like a talisman. "Was he here?"

The receptionist gave a start, fingers hovering over her keyboard as if afraid to touch it. "Yes, but... he just checked out. Maybe five minutes ago. You must have..."

"Driven past him in the car park," Finn finished for her, and already his mind was sprinting ahead, calculating the time lost, the distance gained by Sandler.

"Damn," Amelia muttered under her breath.

Finn's jaw clenched, the frustration a physical weight within him. This was his shot at redemption, at proving himself once more. Every second delayed was another second Sandler had to slip through their fingers.

"Car details?" Finn asked.

"I'm not sure if I should, it might be..." the receptionist started.

"Ugh, we don't have time for this!" Finn said, swiveling the receptionist's antiquated computer screen around. He looked at the car type and registration, memorized them, then turned to Amelia.

"Thank you," Amelia said curtly to the receptionist, turning back toward the entrance, Finn right on her heels.

"I hope you're in the mood for a car chase!" Finn said with a grin as they darted out of the hotel lobby, the automatic doors wheezing behind them in protest.

The crisp air slapped Finn's face as they exited, a harsh reminder of the cold trail they could soon be following if they didn't move fast.

"See if you can put out the word for the number plate," the words were tight, clipped, as though each one cost Finn something to say.

Outside, the gray sky loomed ominously over the car park as they slid into their unmarked police car, its engine coughing to life under Finn's eager start. His fingers gripped the steering wheel, channels of determination etched into his knuckles. The car thrust forward, and they sped on.

Amelia was punching the number plate into the police database on her mobile, her thumb a blur. But Finn's eyes were already scanning, darting between the lines of parked cars, searching for that telltale azure glint of metal.

Something moved towards the road in the distance.

"There!" Amelia pointed.

"Got you," he muttered, eyes locking onto the retreating form of a car that fit the description. It was edging towards the exit, deceptively casual. Finn slammed his foot down on the accelerator, and the vehicle leaped forward like a hound released from its leash.

"Careful, Finn," Amelia cautioned as they shot out of the parking lot, barely avoiding a collision with an unsuspecting hatchback. Her voice was steady, but her hand braced against the dashboard betrayed her concern.

Sandler must have caught on and suddenly sped away, fast and direct along the road downhill, towards a wide open expanse of frozen countryside.

"Can't lose him," Finn grunted, swerving around a slow-moving lorry. The world outside blurred into streaks of muted color as they gained on Sandler's car. Each twist and turn was executed with a precision that spoke of Finn's Special Agent training, yet there was a raw edge to his driving now, something desperate and untamed.

"Where do you think you're going, Sandler?" The words were more growl than question, the hunter's mantra echoing in his head.

"Alive, Finn. We need him alive," Amelia reminded him, her gaze fixed on the shrinking gap between them and their quarry. "And I'd like to be alive, too!"

"Right." His grip on the wheel tightened, resolve steeling within him. If there was even the smallest chance that Sandler had information about Max Vilne, if he could lead them to him so Finn could protect his loved ones, then nothing else mattered.

The chase narrowed to a tunnel, a singular purpose from which he couldn't—wouldn't—deviate.

"Watch it!" Amelia's voice snapped him back just in time to avoid clipping the curb as they took another corner at breakneck speed.

"Got it," Finn replied, though his focus was already leaping ahead, plotting the next move in this deadly game of cat and mouse. There was no room for error, not with so much at stake.

Their car ate up the distance, the roar of the engine a testament to Finn's driving and the urgency that propelled them. He could almost feel the vibrations of Sandler's vehicle in his bones, an echo of the chase that thrummed through his veins.

"Almost there..." The words were half prayer, half promise. Finn Wright would not let this killer slip away, not when justice was finally within reach. "I can nudge him off the road."

The bridge loomed ahead, a narrow steel span arching over the churning river below. Finn's hands were steady as he barreled the car onto the structure, the suspect's vehicle only a breath away, swerving in a desperate bid to shake them.

"Left side, now!" Amelia's command was sharp, her body bracing against the door as Finn veered hard to the left, edging closer to Sandler's fleeing car.

Their vehicles collided with a teeth-rattling crunch, metal screeching against metal. The police car shuddered, threatening to mount the pavement and topple into the water's frenzied grasp. Finn's reflexes kicked in, counter-steering with precision honed in countless pursuits, tires skidding perilously close to the edge where the river roared, hungry for more than rainwater.

"Dammit, Finn, you're being reckless!" Amelia's voice cut through the chaos, her hand gripping the dashboard as if she could somehow will them back from the precipice.

"Vilne might be with him!" Finn began, his jaw clenched and his words unhinged.

"You don't know that!" Her retort was immediate, fierce. "We can't afford to lose control."

"I'm trying to protect—" he started, but the words lodged in his throat, half-formed and laced with desperation.

Amelia shot him a look, her eyes wide with something akin to surprise—or was it realization? In that fleeting glance, there was a silent exchange, a collision of intent and concern that spoke louder than the din around them.

Finn eased off the accelerator momentarily, his chest tight, not from the chase but from the weight of responsibility bearing down on him. In the rear view mirror, he saw Sandler's car gaining distance, slipping further away as they rounded the end of the bridge.

"Focus," Amelia snapped, her gaze returning to the road. "We can't let him get away because we're lying in a ditch."

"Right," Finn muttered, the engine's growl mirroring the frustration coiling within him. He pushed the car forward, chasing the gap that had grown between predator and prey. His mind raced, teeming with scenarios, each one ending with Max Vilne's capture—and the safety of those Finn vowed to shield from harm.

The industrial estate loomed like a sullen behemoth, its silhouette etched against the waning daylight. Finn's grip on the steering wheel was vice-like as he navigated the labyrinth of decaying structures and derelict machinery. The killer's car, a shadowy figure cutting through the desolation, bobbed in and out of view.

"Over there!" Amelia pointed to the left, where a narrow passage promised to swallow Sandler whole.

"Got it!" Finn swerved, tires skidding on slick concrete, the chase hot and unyielding. They barreled into the junkyard, an arena of forgotten metal carcasses stretching toward the sky. Puddles from the day's rain blurred the boundaries between land and water, threatening to pull them into their murky depths.

"Christ," Finn muttered under his breath, maneuvering the car with precision born of old instincts and new urgency. They weaved around heaps of rusted vehicles, each turn an echo of the stakes at play.

"Careful!" Amelia's voice pierced the cacophony of revving engines and crunching gravel.

"Trust me." But even as he said it, doubt gnawed at him. The terrain here was a minefield, the ditches yawning like open graves ready to claim the unwary.

Suddenly, Sandler's car vanished behind a monstrous pile of junk, leaving Finn grasping at fading trails of exhaust. He slammed the brakes, heart thumping a rapid tempo against his ribs—not from exertion, but from the sudden drop in momentum.

"Dammit," he breathed, scanning frantically for any sign of

movement.

"Look, Finn," Amelia touched his arm, her voice steady despite the adrenaline that surely coursed through her as well. "I'll head back to the entrance. If he tries to double back, I can call you."

"Are you sure?" Finn's eyes met hers, reflecting a turbulence that matched the churning waters around them.

"It's the best play we have." She unbuckled her seat belt, resolve etching her features. "Otherwise we could be driving around here four hours and not realize he's miles away out of the place."

"Okay." Finn nodded, reluctantly accepting the division in their partnership. "Be careful, Amelia."

"Always am," she said with a smile, clearly imitating Finn's often used words. With a swift motion, Amelia exited the vehicle, her form swiftly receding into the graveyard of steel and rubber.

Alone now, Finn felt the weight of the hunt settle upon him. This was more than a pursuit; it was a testament to his resolve, to the promise he made himself to never let the darkness win. Restarting the engine, he pulled away, his senses sharpened to the task at hand. The game of cat and mouse had narrowed to a perilous point, and he was all too aware that in this junkyard, every shadow could be a harbinger of danger—or justice delayed.

The metal giants loomed over Finn, their rusted bodies casting long shadows across the labyrinth of scrapped vehicles. He navigated the narrow aisles with a predator's focus, eyes panning for any sign of movement that betrayed Steven Sandler's presence. Water sloshed under the tires, spraying arcs of murky liquid that dappled the car's battered exterior.

"Come on, where are you?" Finn muttered to himself, his knuckles white as he gripped the steering wheel. His gaze flickered to the rear view mirror—nothing but an impenetrable maze behind him.

Suddenly, a glint of sunlight off metal caught his attention. There! A vehicle tucked between two mangled buses, its engine purring like a cornered beast ready to bolt. Without hesitation, Finn accelerated toward it.

"Gotcha," he breathed, the thrill of the chase igniting in his veins.

Sandler's car lurched forward, weaving through the debris with reckless abandon. Finn pushed his own vehicle harder, the suspension groaning in protest as they played a deadly game of tag amongst the carcasses of forgotten journeys.

"Running won't save you, Sandler!" Finn shouted into the void, though his words were lost in the roar of engines and the creak of twisted metal.

He gained ground, the killer's rear bumper within reach, when suddenly Sandler's car disappeared further ahead behind a huge stack of crushed cars. Finn's instincts screamed a warning as he followed—he was driving into a trap. Just as he rounded the corner, his fear materialized. Sandler's car sat idle next to a large, steep drop, a large flood covering the ground in icy, muddy water at its foot. The driver's door was open and a figure stood beside it, grinning, gun aimed and ready.

"Police! Drop the weapon!" Finn yelled, knowing full well Sandler wouldn't comply.

Gunshots rang out, bullets pinging against the hood and shattering the windshield. Finn ducked instinctively, heart pounding, as he floored the accelerator. He aimed straight for Sandler, a desperate bid to end this here and now.

"Dammit, don't make me do this," he whispered, bracing for impact.

But then, something unexpected—a blur of motion from the side. Amelia must have doubled back, having seen the car. Undeterred by danger, she launched herself at Sandler, her body colliding with his in a tangle of limbs and fury. All this as Finn's car hurtled towards them both.

"Amelia!" Finn's pulse spiked, hands jerking the wheel to the left to avoid hitting Amelia. The car skidded on wet gravel, sending a spray of stones into the air as he fought for control.

Finn slammed the brakes, the vehicle fishtailing before it slid down a sharp incline. His world somersaulted into a dizzying plunge, the car nosing down into the icy embrace of a vast watery grave. His ears popped with the pressure as murky water gushed in through the seams of the door, hungrily swallowing the interior of his vehicle. He clawed at the seat belt release, his fingers slipping on the button, panic flaring deep within him.

"Come on, come on!" Finn gasped, pressing the button again and again. His breaths were ragged bursts, white clouds in the chilling water that rose steadily, threatening to silence him forever. But the belt wouldn't give.

Above the surface, muffled by the water that now filled the car, came the sound of gunshots—each one a dull thud against his eardrums. The windscreen starred, lines etching across the glass before it gave way, sending shards into the water like fractured pieces of ice.

"God, no!" he spat out, expecting the cold steel kiss of a bullet next. Instead, the cold touch of death was the water itself, seeping into his clothes, pulling him down. He was now completely submerged and unable to breathe.

He tugged at the seat belt once more, muscles straining, when another sound pierced the watery veil—a gunshot, louder, closer, followed by the sensation of something colliding with the sunken car.

Who's there? He thought, bubbles rising to the surface from his mouth, his last gasp of air escaping. Finn's eyes stung as he tried to see through the dirt-water gloom.

The seat belt still wouldn't release. And now he knew how he would die, cold and alone by the side of a road.

Amelia, he thought. He wished he had told her how he felt. Every other worry in his life melted away but that one. That was his greatest regret.

Finn's lungs burned with the need for oxygen, his vision blurring as he fought against the murky depths. The cold grasp of the water was unyielding, but it was a glimpse of movement within the chaos that caught his gaze—a figure, struggling, contorted in an unnatural dance with death, and yet swimming towards him.

It was Amelia "Go back!" he shouted in the water, bubbles escaping his lips as he recognized her form.

Amelia reached down with her silken white hand and pushed against seat belt release switch. Now, Finn knew the truth. The inside of the car had been twisted by the crash, parts of it jutting out like metal splinters, and the seat belt had jammed with it.

That was when he saw something in Amelia's other hand. She aimed a gun at the seat belt release and pulled the trigger. The sound of the gunshot, warped and strange, sounded, and the seat belt was free.

Amelia help Finn out, his lungs ready to burst if he couldn't get a breath. But as he clambered through the windscreen and was now just inches from the surface, he heard a panicked noise. Turning, he now saw that Amelia was in trouble. Her foot ensnared by the wreckage that had once been their refuge on four wheels. His heart thundered in his ears, not with fear, but with resolute determination.

With all the strength that was left to him, Finn pushed back, climbing into the submerged car once more. He reached her, his fingers tracing the twisted metal that held her captive. It was as if the car itself had turned predator, its steel jaws clamped firmly around her.

In the dim underwater light, he saw Amelia's face, tight with pain and effort. Her eyes met his, a silent understanding passing between them. They had always communicated best without words, two halves of a single purposeful entity.

She tugged at her leg, unable to see from the angle how she was stuck, bubbles streaming upward from the exertion.

Finn looked down and saw the problem. He only had seconds left to live. He had to get this right. Wedging his hands into the small gap between two metal pieces that had locked around Amelia's foot, he shoved his hands forward. The sharp edges bit into his flesh, the iron taste of his own blood mingling with the brackish water. But this was no time for pain or hesitation.

He tensed every muscle in his body and clenched his teeth, and with a Herculean effort, he wrenched the metal apart. The sound of rending steel was lost to the water, but he felt the give as Amelia's foot came free.

They grabbed each other, pulling through the windscreen and then pushing their legs against the car.

Together, they kicked toward the surface, shadows of the junkyard looming over them like specters of a mechanical graveyard. Finn's chest screamed for air, every stroke fueled by adrenaline and the unspoken promise that he would not let the murky depths claim either of them.

So close, Finn thought, his mind clinging to that singular goal as the light above grew brighter, promising life and breath.

They broke the surface, gasping, the world returning in a rush of sound and cold air. Amelia coughed violently, spitting out water, her hand gripping Finn's arm with a strength that belied her ordeal.

"Are you..." Finn began, water streaming from his face.

"Alive," Amelia interrupted, her voice hoarse but steady. "Thanks to you."

They shared a look, one that spoke volumes of the ordeal they had just survived and the bond that had formed between them—a bond not even the steely jaws of death could sever.

Waterlogged and wheezing, Finn felt the pebbled grain of the riverbank beneath his palms as he and Amelia crawled from the river's clutches. The chill of the water was a stark counterpoint to the heat of the chase that still clung to their skin. They were two survivors, wrenching themselves from nature's icy grip, their bodies protesting with every movement.

"Amelia," Finn panted, water streaming from his drenched clothes, his voice barely rising above the sound of the lapping waves. "I... I love you."

She turned to him, her eyes wide, the dim light reflecting off her soaked form. Her lips parted, releasing a breathless chuckle that defied the gravity of their situation. "I know, Finn," she replied, her tone carrying a weight of unsaid words, a mix of gratitude and something deeper.

Finn could feel his pulse in his temples, the adrenaline slowly giving way to a relentless cold that seemed to seep into his bones. But it was not the cold that made him shiver; it was the realization that had crystallized during those desperate moments underwater. He had been willing to trade everything for her safety, and now, in the afterglow of chaos, he understood the magnitude of what they had endured together.

Nearby, the sprawled figure of Steven Sandler lay motionless against the backdrop of scattered debris. His chest rose and fell with shallow breaths, betraying his unconscious state. Amelia's handiwork, no doubt—a testament to her resolve and capability even when facing the barrel of a gun.

"Looks like you took him down," Finn observed with a wry smile, trying to push away the tremor in his voice.

"Couldn't let him take any more shots at you," she said, her gaze flickering toward the inert villain. "Besides, it seemed like the appropriate time for a dramatic entrance. I usually leave that to you."

Despite the gravity of the moment, Finn couldn't help but laugh—a short, sharp release of tension that echoed oddly among the twisted metal sculptures of the junkyard. It was a laugh born not of humor, but of relief; the kind that acknowledged the absurdity of life and death dancing on such a fine edge.

"Never thought I'd say this," he admitted, "but I'm glad you came back and didn't stick to the plan."

"Plans be damned," Amelia retorted, her voice laced with warmth. "It's the strangest thing, I just had a feeling in my gut that I should come back or... Or I'd regret it for the rest of my life."

They helped each other to stand, limbs heavy and uncooperative, the world tilting slightly as they found their footing. As they leaned on each other for support, their silhouettes cast long shadows under the moonlight, intertwined and indistinguishable.

"Let's get out of here," Amelia suggested, her gaze meeting his. There was a steely determination in her eyes, the same determination that had driven her through the murky waters and into the fray.

Finn tried to stand up and then sat back down. "If you don't mind, I might stay here for a bit. It's been one hell of a day."

EPILOGUE

Finn's breath formed a misty veil in the chill air, the scent of oil and metal lingering as he sat at the back of an ambulance, the clamor of the junkyard now replaced by the urgent symphony of police radios and bustling officers. A warm blanket was draped over his shoulders, the fabric rough against his skin, a stark reminder that shock had a grip on him. He glanced to his side where Inspector Amelia Winters sat, her presence like a warm fire to him.

"I know I already said it, but thank you," he murmured, his voice gravelly, eyes not quite meeting hers. "For... back there."

Amelia gave a small, affirmative nod, her gaze scanning the scene before settling back on him. "We saved each other, Finn. That's what partners do, isn't it?" Her tone held a note of camaraderie that was hard to ignore.

Finn watched a constable dash by, his feet kicking up bits of gravel. In this pandemonium, his mind surprisingly found clarity. As he looked at Amelia, the realization seeped into him like rain into parched soil. His feelings for Demi, tangled and frayed as they were, paled in comparison to the solid partnership he'd built with Amelia. It was time to untie the knots of the past and consider a future unburdened by old regrets. He didn't want to hurt Demi, but it was time to move on.

"Amelia," he started, his voice steadier now, the decision cementing itself in his mind. "When all this is over, would—"

A sudden interruption cut his words short, but the resolve within him remained unshaken. Finn knew that once the dust settled and the adrenaline ceased its flow, he would ask Amelia on a date. A simple question, yet one that marked a new beginning.

Through the discordant symphony of radio chatter and the diesel growl of arriving vehicles, Finn's gaze followed the subdued figure of the killer. He was a gaunt silhouette against the flashing blue lights, his steps shackled but oddly buoyant as if he still harbored some secret delight in his capture. Handcuffs glinted dully on his wrists, a metallic punctuation to his chapter of terror.

"Looks like Steven Sandler was our guy after all," Amelia commented dryly, her eyes tracking the man she'd hunted with such tenacious resolve. "Though no connection to Vilne...

"I'm not sure about that," Finn replied, the weight of his own past briefly surfacing in his tone. He watched intently as the constables loaded the handcuffed man into a car. The slam of the door echoed, a satisfying conclusion to the pursuit. "The man is an historian. Who gave him that gun?"

"You still think Vilne is connected?" Amelia asked.

"I just can't let that go," Finn added, tension unspooling within him as the threat receded with each step the officers took.

A familiar voice cut through the muddle of activity, bringing with it a semblance of normalcy. "Well, if it isn't Houdini himself. Should've known you'd turn up at the deep end without so much as a snorkel."

Rob's tall frame came into view, a smirk playing across his features. His light-hearted jab did little to mask the relief in his eyes as they rested on Finn and then Amelia.

"Swimming wasn't exactly on my agenda for today," Finn shot back with a half-smile, shifting under the blanket's warmth. "But I'm not one to shy away from a spontaneous dip."

"Spontaneous? That's one word for it." Rob chuckled, scratching his head.

"Don't listen to him, Chief. He swims like a stone," Amelia quipped, her posture relaxed despite the remnants of adrenaline that Finn could sense in her quick wit.

"Breaststroke, backstroke, dog paddle—I would've made it work," Finn said. His gaze lingered on Amelia. She smiled, and he wondered what she truly thought of him.

"Whatever stroke you fancy, mate," Rob remarked, a grin spreading across his face. "I'm just glad you both are here, relatively dry and in one piece."

Amid the metallic tang of oil and rust, Rob leaned against the bonnet of a police car, his arms folded as he surveyed the scene. "We'll dig into our friend's history," he said, nodding toward the departing vehicle that held the subdued killer. "Preliminary intel suggests we're dealing with an antique smuggling ring."

"Antiques? You mean Arron Reinhardt?" Amelia raised an eyebrow and a grin. She shifted her weight from one foot to the other, the gravel beneath her boots crunching in quiet protest.

Finn laughed. "We're way ahead of you, Rob."

"Any chance this ties back to Vilne, though?" Amelia asked. "Finn thinks the gun is suspect."

"I could see him providing the gun and pushing the Historian to do what he did, but I have no proof yet. I hate that he's still out there," Finn said. "None of us are safe until he's behind bars."

"There's nothing solid yet." Rob's eyes met Amelia's with a steady resolve. "If there's a link, we'll find it. His face has been plastered across the news by now, so hopefully we'll have a lead soon."

The conversation paused as a constable rushed past, a blur of hi-vis against the backdrop of the junkyard's decrepitude. Finn looked up, catching Amelia's gaze. She offered him another smile, but then averted her gaze like a teenager.

There was an awkward silence, which Rob seemed aware of and in need to fill. "We're turning over every stone, Finn, so it won't be long until we catch Vilne."

"Turning over every stone, huh?" Finn leaned forward, elbows resting on his knees. "I should warn you, I've been known to cause a landslide now and then."

"Is that so?" Amelia crossed her arms, a playful glint in her eye. "Well, just try not to bury us all under it like you did with your driving."

"My driving was fine, it's these British cars," Finn replied, his voice light despite the gravity of their situation. "But I'll be on my best behavior from now on."

"Good, because I don't fancy digging myself out of another one of your messes," Rob interjected, his wry smile returning. "Especially if it involves paperwork."

"Paperwork," Finn scoffed. "Now that's the real crime here."

"Agreed," Amelia chuckled, the sound mingling with the distant chatter of constables and the occasional clatter of equipment being moved.

The evening air was sharp with the tang of metal and oil as the night sky began to cloud over, high above the skeletal remains of discarded vehicles. Finn's breath formed fleeting clouds themselves, dissipating into the darkness. He traced patterns on the woolen blanket draped over his shoulders, a half-hearted attempt to distract himself from the gnawing uncertainty that clawed at his insides.

"Chief!" A constable's voice cut through the murmur of conversation, urgent and tinged with an unmistakable edge of alarm. The young officer's boots crunched over gravel as he navigated between the police cars, making a beeline for Rob.

Rob turned, his expression tightening as he took in the constable's pale face. "What is it?"

"It's your friend, Demi," the constable panted, chest heaving from exertion. "She's... she's gone, sir."

Finn's head snapped up, his pulse thundering in his ears as he pushed off the ambulance, the blanket slipping unnoticed from his shoulders. "Gone? What do you mean, gone?" The question was a growl, the words laced with a cold dread that settled heavy in his stomach.

"Both guards down," the constable continued, struggling to regain his breath. "Knocked out by gas. When they came to... she was just... vanished."

"Gas?" Amelia echoed, her brow furrowing in concentration. "That doesn't sound like amateur work."

"Nothing about this is amateur," Finn muttered, the gears in his mind whirring with frantic energy. He knew the ugliness that lurked in the shadows of Max Vilne's mind, the lengths to which the man would go for his perverse sense of vengeance. He still had deep feelings for Demi and always would, and to think of her at the mercy of his touch made Finn feel sick.

Standing, Finn towered over the huddle, his figure rigid with resolve. "We need to find her. Now." His voice was steel, the command unmistakable. Finn didn't wait for affirmation; he was already striding toward the nearest vehicle, keys jangling from his pocket.

"Whatever it takes," he added, not looking back. "Because if we don't, Max Vilne will..." He let the sentence hang, the implication more terrifying than any words he could muster.

Amelia exchanged a look with Rob, then followed closely behind Finn.

"Let's mobilize," Rob ordered, already motioning for officers to fall into step. "Every second counts."

The junkyard, once a place of forgotten things, had become the crutch of a desperate night—one that Finn knew might swallow them all.

NOW AVAILABLE!

WHEN YOU'RE SILENT
(A Finn Wright FBI Suspense Thriller—Book Six)

FBI Special Agent Finn Wright, put on leave after bending too many rules, is needed by his detective friend when descendants of royalty become the latest targets of a ruthless serial killer. Can he decipher the historical clues to prevent another execution before it's too late?

"A masterpiece of thriller and mystery."
—Books and Movie Reviews, Roberto Mattos (re Once Gone)

WHEN YOU'RE SILENT is book #6 in a long-anticipated new series by #1 bestseller and USA Today bestselling author Blake Pierce, whose bestseller Once Gone (a free download) has received over 7,000 five star ratings and reviews. The series begins with WHEN YOU'RE MINE (book #1).

Recently put on leave and divorced after he caught his wife cheating on him, Finn needs a fresh start in life. He thought a visit to an old friend in a tranquil small town in England would be a good step—until his friend needs his expertise with a series of murders in spectacular estates. With the local police chief impressed, Finn is asked to stay on, as they need his help.

As Finn's eyes are opened to a world of storied wealth, history and privacy, he realizes that he has much to learn—but that killers are universal….

A page-turning crime thriller featuring a brilliant and tortured FBI agent, the Finn Wright series is a riveting mystery, packed with non-stop action, suspense, twists and turns, revelations, and driven by a breakneck pace that will keep you flipping pages late into the night. Fans of Rachel Caine, Teresa Driscoll and Robert Dugoni are sure to fall in love.

Future books in the series are also available!

"An edge of your seat thriller in a new series that keeps you turning pages! ...So many twists, turns and red herrings... I can't wait to see what happens next."
—Reader review (Her Last Wish)

"A strong, complex story about two FBI agents trying to stop a serial killer. If you want an author to capture your attention and have you guessing, yet trying to put the pieces together, Pierce is your author!"
—Reader review (Her Last Wish)

"A typical Blake Pierce twisting, turning, roller coaster ride suspense thriller. Will have you turning the pages to the last sentence of the last chapter!!!"
—Reader review (City of Prey)

"Right from the start we have an unusual protagonist that I haven't seen done in this genre before. The action is nonstop... A very atmospheric novel that will keep you turning pages well into the wee hours."
—Reader review (City of Prey)

"Everything that I look for in a book... a great plot, interesting characters, and grabs your interest right away. The book moves along at a breakneck pace and stays that way until the end. Now on go I to book two!"
—Reader review (Girl, Alone)

"Exciting, heart pounding, edge of your seat book... a must read for mystery and suspense readers!"
—Reader review (Girl, Alone)

Blake Pierce

Blake Pierce is the USA Today bestselling author of the RILEY PAGE mystery series, which includes seventeen books. Blake Pierce is also the author of the MACKENZIE WHITE mystery series, comprising fourteen books; of the AVERY BLACK mystery series, comprising six books; of the KERI LOCKE mystery series, comprising five books; of the MAKING OF RILEY PAIGE mystery series, comprising six books; of the KATE WISE mystery series, comprising seven books; of the CHLOE FINE psychological suspense mystery, comprising six books; of the JESSIE HUNT psychological suspense thriller series, comprising thirty-five books (and counting); of the AU PAIR psychological suspense thriller series, comprising three books; of the ZOE PRIME mystery series, comprising six books; of the ADELE SHARP mystery series, comprising sixteen books, of the EUROPEAN VOYAGE cozy mystery series, comprising six books; of the LAURA FROST FBI suspense thriller, comprising eleven books; of the ELLA DARK FBI suspense thriller, comprising twenty-one books (and counting); of the A YEAR IN EUROPE cozy mystery series, comprising nine books, of the AVA GOLD mystery series, comprising six books; of the RACHEL GIFT mystery series, comprising thirteen books (and counting); of the VALERIE LAW mystery series, comprising nine books; of the PAIGE KING mystery series, comprising eight books; of the MAY MOORE mystery series, comprising eleven books; of the CORA SHIELDS mystery series, comprising eight books; of the NICKY LYONS mystery series, comprising eight books, of the CAMI LARK mystery series, comprising ten books; of the AMBER YOUNG mystery series, comprising seven books (and counting); of the DAISY FORTUNE mystery series, comprising five books; of the FIONA RED mystery series, comprising eleven books (and counting); of the FAITH BOLD mystery series, comprising eleven books (and counting); of the JULIETTE HART mystery series, comprising five books (and counting); of the MORGAN CROSS mystery series, comprising nine books (and counting); of the FINN WRIGHT mystery series, comprising five books (and counting); of the new SHEILA STONE suspense thriller series, comprising five books (and counting); and of the new RACHEL BLACKWOOD suspense thriller series, comprising five books (and counting).

An avid reader and lifelong fan of the mystery and thriller genres, Blake loves to hear from you, so please feel free to visit www.blakepierceauthor.com to learn more and stay in touch.

BOOKS BY BLAKE PIERCE

RACHEL BLACKWOOD SUSPENSE THRILLER
NOT THIS WAY (Book #1)
NOT THIS TIME (Book #2)
NOT THIS CLOSE (Book #3)
NOT THIS ROAD (Book #4)
NOT THIS LATE (Book #5)

SHEILA STONE SUSPENSE THRILLER
SILENT GIRL (Book #1)
SILENT TRAIL (Book #2)
SILENT NIGHT (Book #3)
SILENT HOUSE (Book #4)
SILENT SCREAM (Book #5)

FINN WRIGHT MYSTERY SERIES
WHEN YOU'RE MINE (Book #1)
WHEN YOU'RE SAFE (Book #2)
WHEN YOU'RE CLOSE (Book #3)
WHEN YOU'RE SLEEPING (Book #4)
WHEN YOU'RE SANE (Book #5)

MORGAN CROSS MYSTERY SERIES
FOR YOU (Book #1)
FOR RAGE (Book #2)
FOR LUST (Book #3)
FOR WRATH (Book #4)
FOREVER (Book #5)
FOR US (Book #6)
FOR NOW (Book #7)
FOR ONCE (Book #8)
FOR ETERNITY (Book #9)

JULIETTE HART MYSTERY SERIES
NOTHING TO FEAR (Book #1)
NOTHING THERE (Book #2)

NOTHING WATCHING (Book #3)
NOTHING HIDING (Book #4)
NOTHING LEFT (Book #5)

FAITH BOLD MYSTERY SERIES
SO LONG (Book #1)
SO COLD (Book #2)
SO SCARED (Book #3)
SO NORMAL (Book #4)
SO FAR GONE (Book #5)
SO LOST (Book #6)
SO ALONE (Book #7)
SO FORGOTTEN (Book #8)
SO INSANE (Book #9)
SO SMITTEN (Book #10)
SO SIMPLE (Book #11)

FIONA RED MYSTERY SERIES
LET HER GO (Book #1)
LET HER BE (Book #2)
LET HER HOPE (Book #3)
LET HER WISH (Book #4)
LET HER LIVE (Book #5)
LET HER RUN (Book #6)
LET HER HIDE (Book #7)
LET HER BELIEVE (Book #8)
LET HER FORGET (Book #9)
LET HER TRY (Book #10)
LET HER PLAY (Book #11)

DAISY FORTUNE MYSTERY SERIES
NEED YOU (Book #1)
CLAIM YOU (Book #2)
CRAVE YOU (Book #3)
CHOOSE YOU (Book #4)
CHASE YOU (Book #5)

AMBER YOUNG MYSTERY SERIES
ABSENT PITY (Book #1)
ABSENT REMORSE (Book #2)

ABSENT FEELING (Book #3)
ABSENT MERCY (Book #4)
ABSENT REASON (Book #5)
ABSENT SANITY (Book #6)
ABSENT LIFE (Book #7)

CAMI LARK MYSTERY SERIES
JUST ME (Book #1)
JUST OUTSIDE (Book #2)
JUST RIGHT (Book #3)
JUST FORGET (Book #4)
JUST ONCE (Book #5)
JUST HIDE (Book #6)
JUST NOW (Book #7)
JUST HOPE (Book #8)
JUST LEAVE (Book #9)
JUST TONIGHT (Book #10)

NICKY LYONS MYSTERY SERIES
ALL MINE (Book #1)
ALL HIS (Book #2)
ALL HE SEES (Book #3)
ALL ALONE (Book #4)
ALL FOR ONE (Book #5)
ALL HE TAKES (Book #6)
ALL FOR ME (Book #7)
ALL IN (Book #8)

CORA SHIELDS MYSTERY SERIES
UNDONE (Book #1)
UNWANTED (Book #2)
UNHINGED (Book #3)
UNSAID (Book #4)
UNGLUED (Book #5)
UNSTABLE (Book #6)
UNKNOWN (Book #7)
UNAWARE (Book #8)

MAY MOORE SUSPENSE THRILLER
NEVER RUN (Book #1)

NEVER TELL (Book #2)
NEVER LIVE (Book #3)
NEVER HIDE (Book #4)
NEVER FORGIVE (Book #5)
NEVER AGAIN (Book #6)
NEVER LOOK BACK (Book #7)
NEVER FORGET (Book #8)
NEVER LET GO (Book #9)
NEVER PRETEND (Book #10)
NEVER HESITATE (Book #11)

PAIGE KING MYSTERY SERIES
THE GIRL HE PINED (Book #1)
THE GIRL HE CHOSE (Book #2)
THE GIRL HE TOOK (Book #3)
THE GIRL HE WISHED (Book #4)
THE GIRL HE CROWNED (Book #5)
THE GIRL HE WATCHED (Book #6)
THE GIRL HE WANTED (Book #7)
THE GIRL HE CLAIMED (Book #8)

VALERIE LAW MYSTERY SERIES
NO MERCY (Book #1)
NO PITY (Book #2)
NO FEAR (Book #3)
NO SLEEP (Book #4)
NO QUARTER (Book #5)
NO CHANCE (Book #6)
NO REFUGE (Book #7)
NO GRACE (Book #8)
NO ESCAPE (Book #9)

RACHEL GIFT MYSTERY SERIES
HER LAST WISH (Book #1)
HER LAST CHANCE (Book #2)
HER LAST HOPE (Book #3)
HER LAST FEAR (Book #4)
HER LAST CHOICE (Book #5)
HER LAST BREATH (Book #6)
HER LAST MISTAKE (Book #7)

HER LAST DESIRE (Book #8)
HER LAST REGRET (Book #9)
HER LAST HOUR (Book #10)
HER LAST SHOT (Book #11)
HER LAST PRAYER (Book #12)
HER LAST LIE (Book #13)

AVA GOLD MYSTERY SERIES
CITY OF PREY (Book #1)
CITY OF FEAR (Book #2)
CITY OF BONES (Book #3)
CITY OF GHOSTS (Book #4)
CITY OF DEATH (Book #5)
CITY OF VICE (Book #6)

A YEAR IN EUROPE
A MURDER IN PARIS (Book #1)
DEATH IN FLORENCE (Book #2)
VENGEANCE IN VIENNA (Book #3)
A FATALITY IN SPAIN (Book #4)

ELLA DARK FBI SUSPENSE THRILLER
GIRL, ALONE (Book #1)
GIRL, TAKEN (Book #2)
GIRL, HUNTED (Book #3)
GIRL, SILENCED (Book #4)
GIRL, VANISHED (Book 5)
GIRL ERASED (Book #6)
GIRL, FORSAKEN (Book #7)
GIRL, TRAPPED (Book #8)
GIRL, EXPENDABLE (Book #9)
GIRL, ESCAPED (Book #10)
GIRL, HIS (Book #11)
GIRL, LURED (Book #12)
GIRL, MISSING (Book #13)
GIRL, UNKNOWN (Book #14)
GIRL, DECEIVED (Book #15)
GIRL, FORLORN (Book #16)
GIRL, REMADE (Book #17)
GIRL, BETRAYED (Book #18)

GIRL, BOUND (Book #19)
GIRL, REFORMED (Book #20)
GIRL, REBORN (Book #21)

LAURA FROST FBI SUSPENSE THRILLER
ALREADY GONE (Book #1)
ALREADY SEEN (Book #2)
ALREADY TRAPPED (Book #3)
ALREADY MISSING (Book #4)
ALREADY DEAD (Book #5)
ALREADY TAKEN (Book #6)
ALREADY CHOSEN (Book #7)
ALREADY LOST (Book #8)
ALREADY HIS (Book #9)
ALREADY LURED (Book #10)
ALREADY COLD (Book #11)

EUROPEAN VOYAGE COZY MYSTERY SERIES
MURDER (AND BAKLAVA) (Book #1)
DEATH (AND APPLE STRUDEL) (Book #2)
CRIME (AND LAGER) (Book #3)
MISFORTUNE (AND GOUDA) (Book #4)
CALAMITY (AND A DANISH) (Book #5)
MAYHEM (AND HERRING) (Book #6)

ADELE SHARP MYSTERY SERIES
LEFT TO DIE (Book #1)
LEFT TO RUN (Book #2)
LEFT TO HIDE (Book #3)
LEFT TO KILL (Book #4)
LEFT TO MURDER (Book #5)
LEFT TO ENVY (Book #6)
LEFT TO LAPSE (Book #7)
LEFT TO VANISH (Book #8)
LEFT TO HUNT (Book #9)
LEFT TO FEAR (Book #10)
LEFT TO PREY (Book #11)
LEFT TO LURE (Book #12)
LEFT TO CRAVE (Book #13)
LEFT TO LOATHE (Book #14)

LEFT TO HARM (Book #15)
LEFT TO RUIN (Book #16)

THE AU PAIR SERIES
ALMOST GONE (Book#1)
ALMOST LOST (Book #2)
ALMOST DEAD (Book #3)

ZOE PRIME MYSTERY SERIES
FACE OF DEATH (Book#1)
FACE OF MURDER (Book #2)
FACE OF FEAR (Book #3)
FACE OF MADNESS (Book #4)
FACE OF FURY (Book #5)
FACE OF DARKNESS (Book #6)

A JESSIE HUNT PSYCHOLOGICAL SUSPENSE SERIES
THE PERFECT WIFE (Book #1)
THE PERFECT BLOCK (Book #2)
THE PERFECT HOUSE (Book #3)
THE PERFECT SMILE (Book #4)
THE PERFECT LIE (Book #5)
THE PERFECT LOOK (Book #6)
THE PERFECT AFFAIR (Book #7)
THE PERFECT ALIBI (Book #8)
THE PERFECT NEIGHBOR (Book #9)
THE PERFECT DISGUISE (Book #10)
THE PERFECT SECRET (Book #11)
THE PERFECT FAÇADE (Book #12)
THE PERFECT IMPRESSION (Book #13)
THE PERFECT DECEIT (Book #14)
THE PERFECT MISTRESS (Book #15)
THE PERFECT IMAGE (Book #16)
THE PERFECT VEIL (Book #17)
THE PERFECT INDISCRETION (Book #18)
THE PERFECT RUMOR (Book #19)
THE PERFECT COUPLE (Book #20)
THE PERFECT MURDER (Book #21)
THE PERFECT HUSBAND (Book #22)
THE PERFECT SCANDAL (Book #23)

THE PERFECT MASK (Book #24)
THE PERFECT RUSE (Book #25)
THE PERFECT VENEER (Book #26)
THE PERFECT PEOPLE (Book #27)
THE PERFECT WITNESS (Book #28)
THE PERFECT APPEARANCE (Book #29)
THE PERFECT TRAP (Book #30)
THE PERFECT EXPRESSION (Book #31)
THE PERFECT ACCOMPLICE (Book #32)
THE PERFECT SHOW (Book #33)
THE PERFECT POISE (Book #34)
THE PERFECT CROWD (Book #35)

CHLOE FINE PSYCHOLOGICAL SUSPENSE SERIES
NEXT DOOR (Book #1)
A NEIGHBOR'S LIE (Book #2)
CUL DE SAC (Book #3)
SILENT NEIGHBOR (Book #4)
HOMECOMING (Book #5)
TINTED WINDOWS (Book #6)

KATE WISE MYSTERY SERIES
IF SHE KNEW (Book #1)
IF SHE SAW (Book #2)
IF SHE RAN (Book #3)
IF SHE HID (Book #4)
IF SHE FLED (Book #5)
IF SHE FEARED (Book #6)
IF SHE HEARD (Book #7)

THE MAKING OF RILEY PAIGE SERIES
WATCHING (Book #1)
WAITING (Book #2)
LURING (Book #3)
TAKING (Book #4)
STALKING (Book #5)
KILLING (Book #6)

RILEY PAIGE MYSTERY SERIES
ONCE GONE (Book #1)

ONCE TAKEN (Book #2)
ONCE CRAVED (Book #3)
ONCE LURED (Book #4)
ONCE HUNTED (Book #5)
ONCE PINED (Book #6)
ONCE FORSAKEN (Book #7)
ONCE COLD (Book #8)
ONCE STALKED (Book #9)
ONCE LOST (Book #10)
ONCE BURIED (Book #11)
ONCE BOUND (Book #12)
ONCE TRAPPED (Book #13)
ONCE DORMANT (Book #14)
ONCE SHUNNED (Book #15)
ONCE MISSED (Book #16)
ONCE CHOSEN (Book #17)

MACKENZIE WHITE MYSTERY SERIES
BEFORE HE KILLS (Book #1)
BEFORE HE SEES (Book #2)
BEFORE HE COVETS (Book #3)
BEFORE HE TAKES (Book #4)
BEFORE HE NEEDS (Book #5)
BEFORE HE FEELS (Book #6)
BEFORE HE SINS (Book #7)
BEFORE HE HUNTS (Book #8)
BEFORE HE PREYS (Book #9)
BEFORE HE LONGS (Book #10)
BEFORE HE LAPSES (Book #11)
BEFORE HE ENVIES (Book #12)
BEFORE HE STALKS (Book #13)
BEFORE HE HARMS (Book #14)

AVERY BLACK MYSTERY SERIES
CAUSE TO KILL (Book #1)
CAUSE TO RUN (Book #2)
CAUSE TO HIDE (Book #3)
CAUSE TO FEAR (Book #4)
CAUSE TO SAVE (Book #5)
CAUSE TO DREAD (Book #6)

KERI LOCKE MYSTERY SERIES
A TRACE OF DEATH (Book #1)
A TRACE OF MURDER (Book #2)
A TRACE OF VICE (Book #3)
A TRACE OF CRIME (Book #4)
A TRACE OF HOPE (Book #5)

Made in United States
North Haven, CT
07 January 2025